MERRIE

Vivian Schurfranz

SCHOLASTIC INC.
New York Toronto London Auckland Sydney

To Clarence
The man with the "comma" touch

ISBN 0-590-41000-8

12 11 10 9 8 7 6 5 4 3 2 1   7 8 9/8 0 1 2/9

Printed in the U.S.A.   01

First Scholastic printing, August 1987

MERRIE

A *SUNFIRE* Book

SUNFIRE

Chapter One

FEAR knotted Merrie Courtland's stomach as she shifted her cramped muscles beneath the heavy canvas of the longboat where she was hiding. She prayed no one had heard her. Seven days she'd been hiding. She wondered how she had had the nerve to smuggle aboard the *Mayflower*. Heaven help her if she were discovered! She'd heard the Pilgrims scorned and shunned anyone who didn't believe as they did. The constant up and down motion of the boat and the damp coldness of the canvas exhausted her. She wondered if she had slept as much as fifteen hours since she had stolen on board. With a stab of fright she remembered the night before when she had had to press her hand over her mouth to keep from screaming. Something alive had crawled in with her, and she knew it was a rat! What a relief it had been to discover the ship's cat burrowing at her feet.

The memory of her home at Courtland Manor caused her eyes to fill with tears. She thought longingly of her own bedroom with the lovely ruffled-top canopy bed, its soft mattress and the satin coverlet, which matched the rose-colored drapes of the high windows. How she wished she were sitting at her small oak desk writing a letter to Nancy Bates in London, her best friend. And she remembered her clothes! Now all she had to her name was the red wool dress on her back and its matching cloak. At Courtland Manor her closet had almost overflowed with silk and satin dresses. She pushed cautiously at the damp-smelling canvas over her head, thinking of her dressing table at home filled with perfumes from Paris. Why was life so unfair? She moved her slender shoulders slightly and gingerly lifted the canvas to peer out.

Merrie watched as Christopher Jones, captain of the *Mayflower*, joined Miles Standish and John Alden at the rail, pleased that although she'd only been at sea seven days, she already could identify quite a few of the passengers and crew. Of course, she realized she hadn't seen everyone. If only she could move about as freely as the three men at the ship's rail who looked down at the heaving Atlantic Ocean! She almost groaned, feeling every ache in her body. She'd be glad when night fell and she could once again prowl the deck. In her pacing she'd measured the deck of the *Mayflower*. Ninety feet from stem to stern and twenty feet in the beam.

Suddenly the two lively Billington boys, Francis and Johnny, bounced up onto the deck. They were always causing trouble, and Captain Jones had more than once threatened to toss them overboard. Overboard. She shuddered. He was only joking, of course, but what would the captain do to a stowaway?

Hastily, Merrie ducked beneath the canvas. Although she remained silent, she was certain the boys could hear her pounding heart. Closing her eyes tightly, she vowed to sleep the rest of the day away, but her thoughts kept drifting back to England. Had it really been a whole week since she'd run away from Courtland Manor to this creaking ship?

From the moment her father had ordered her to marry Jeremiah Farmingham, a pudgy middle-aged merchant, her world had turned topsy-turvy. But what was she getting into by leaving home? She breathed deeply. No, she couldn't stay at Courtland Manor. Anything would be better than being forced to marry Jeremiah. She had tried everything to persuade her father to change his mind and thought he'd easily give in, as he usually did. But this time he'd been stubborn.

She'd never forget his stern tone when he'd said, "You will marry Jeremiah Farmingham on your sixteenth birthday!" Since she wouldn't be sixteen until next year, March 27, 1621, she probably should have stayed. Anything could have happened in seven months! She turned restlessly. She'd never sleep for thinking about it. But she finally drifted off.

When she next peered out, it was pitch-dark.

Taking her fine wool cloak with the fox fur hood and collar, Merrie looked cautiously about before she stepped out on deck. She drew in a lungful of fresh sea air; the brisk breeze refreshed her. She pulled her hood closely about her face, revelling in the night walk, the chance to stretch her legs and nibble on an apple while the passengers slept. In the yellow light of the harvest moon the three masts and six sails looked gloriously golden.

She threw her apple core overboard into the black waves below and thought of the manor where she'd had everything she desired. Her mouth watered when she thought of Matilda's roast beef stew. Their housekeeper was the most wonderful cook in the world.

Her father had always given her anything she'd wanted, including fancy clothes and fancy balls. Anything, that is, until she'd reached her sixteenth birthday. Well, she wouldn't marry someone she didn't love! Her father had always said she was too headstrong and pampered for her own good, and she guessed this latest escapade proved it. Even Jeremiah Farmingham might be better than this creaking old ship! She shook her head. No, never Jeremiah Farmingham. She had done the right thing. Her heart skipped a beat. But had she? She no longer felt in control of her life. She only felt like a scared little girl!

Merrie turned her face into the wind and tucked back a strand of hair that blew loosely across her face. Her father had said her hair shone like shimmering gold, even in the dark. Oh, Father, she thought, I miss you. Why am I going to this new land? A land where I have no friends and where Indians lie in wait?

She'd heard stories of the Lost Colony in Virginia. Those colonists had simply vanished, never to be heard from again. What if the same thing happened to the colonists she was now with?

Then there was Jamestown. Nine out of ten settlers had died within a year. Of the twelve hundred who had gone out in 1619, a thousand were dead by 1620.

She knew the Pilgrims were tough enough to defy King James and the Church of England. She hoped they were tough enough to survive in the New World. For twelve years they'd been living in Holland, where they could worship as they pleased, but she'd heard they had become alarmed when their children began to speak Dutch and adopt Dutch customs.

The Separatists, as they were called because they had separated from the English Church, craved a land of freedom where they could speak their own language, follow their own ways, and set up their own government based on religion. She hoped they'd realize their dreams. But would they accept her? Suddenly she heard a sailor singing an off-key sea chantey. Hastily she ducked back to her hiding place, yanking the tarpaulin over her head. She mustn't be found. What if they reversed course and took her back to England, dumping her off at the nearest port.

Closer and closer came the voice:

> "Tell 'em all, tell 'em all,
> Gallowsbirds all, gallowsbirds all,
> Great and small, great and small,
> One and all, one and all."

The song was followed by a whistling of the same tune. Then, to her horror, Merrie felt the canvas torn back and heard the whistling abruptly stop.

"What the. . .!?" The lantern came nearer, and she shrank back. "A stowaway!" The sailor's pugnacious face came close. "What do you think you're doing?" he asked angrily.

Merrie tried to answer, but no words came. Her brown eyes darkened with fear.

Hands on narrow hips, the muscular sailor frowned, surveying her disapprovingly. "A stowaway!" he repeated in disbelief, his eyes flashing angrily in the golden glow of the moon.

Dumbly she nodded, wishing she could make this arrogant sailor disappear.

"Get out of there!" he ordered brusquely. "What will Captain Jones say about this?" He shoved back his knitted cap in perplexity, revealing spiky red hair.

Merrie's palms were sweaty and her knees so weak she couldn't move.

"Come on!" he commanded roughly, gripping her wrist. "Out!" The corners of his mouth turned down even further when he examined her tumbled long hair, her expensive red dress, and her soft leather shoes.

"Oh, please," she gasped, panic forcing the words out, "don't tell the captain about me."

His brows shot upward, and his square jaw tightened. "Of course I'm telling my captain," he growled, eyeing her suspiciously.

"Please don't," she begged. "He'll take me back to England."

The seaman snorted. "I doubt that. What he should do, though, is clap you in chain irons!"

She bit her underlip to keep it from trembling.

"Who are you?" he snapped.

"M-Merrie Courtland," she stammered.

"Merrie Courtland," he repeated, and he folded his brawny arms over his barrel chest, cocking his head. "Pretty fancy lady, aren't you?"

She stared at him, wondering if she should argue further, but by his rakish appearance — his cutoff trousers, bare feet, full-sleeved shirt, and the crimson scarf tied about his sturdy neck — she knew it wouldn't do any good. Was he enjoying her predicament?

"So why did you think you could stow away on an overcrowded ship?" he barked, hooking his thumbs in his wide leather belt.

"I had to," she said, and breathlessly told

7

him about Jeremiah Farmingham. When she'd finished, she gazed at him hopefully. Perhaps he'd be sympathetic after all, and not give her away.

But the red-headed sailor only shook his head and clamped his callused hand over hers. "You can tell your sad story to the captain." He chuckled mirthlessly. "See if it'll do you any good!"

Captain Christopher Jones, the skipper of the *Mayflower*, was indeed angry to find Merrie on board, but he wasn't as mean as the sailor. He certainly didn't sympathize with her, but he didn't yell at her, either. After lecturing her sternly Captain Jones scratched his gray hair, turned to his crewman, and said, "Luke, take Mistress Courtland below to William Brewster. Let the Saints decide where she's to sleep."

Luke nodded, roughly taking Merrie's elbow.

Leading her below, he knocked on a cabin door and was greeted by an elderly gentleman. "Luke, come in," the man said.

"Mr. Brewster," Luke acknowledged, pushing Merrie forward.

Puzzled, Mr. Brewster glanced from Luke to Merrie. Merrie could scarcely meet his eyes and was only dimly aware of the four men who sat behind him with a map on the table.

Luke jerked his thumb in Merrie's direction. "We found a stowaway on board, sir," he growled, giving Merrie a surly look. "Captain Jones wants you to find a bunk for her."

He touched two fingers to his forehead in a salute. "Got to get back on deck, Mr. Brewster." Luke shot one last look at Merrie, then he left, closing the door.

Mr. Brewster, stroking his beard, looked at her sadly. "What's your name?"

"Merrie Courtland, sir," she replied.

"Age?"

"Fifteen."

"Well, Merrie, you pose quite a hardship for everyone on board. I'm Master William Brewster, and I don't have much time for you." He quickly checked a wall chart and muttered, "Thirty-five Pilgrims and sixty-seven other passengers and thirty crewmen! No one is going to be happy to see you!" For a moment he paused. "I'll put you in bunk eighteen with Constanta."

She shifted her feet, too tongue-tied to reply.

"Well, hurry on, girl. Go down the gangway and turn left."

Merrie whirled about, eager to be out of the cabin. The men at the table stared at her as if she were a strange creature.

"One more thing," Master Brewster said. "Ask Mistress Brewster what you can do to earn your keep. Perhaps you can help with the cooking or mending." With these words he dismissed her as if she were so much excess baggage — which she supposed she was.

"Master Brewster," a tall, sour-faced man said in an oily tone, "just a minute." He rose to tower over Merrie, and sneered, "See to it that this intruder doesn't come skulking about when the Pilgrims are at their prayers or singing psalms."

Master Brewster turned slightly. "Now, Master Oliver Loomis, the girl looks terrified enough. We'll see that she's made useful on board."

Mr. Loomis bared his yellow teeth, and his eyes were cold. He hissed, "Mistress Courtland, you're an evil girl for stealing on board! Never forget you're a 'Stranger'!"

Merrie backed against the ship's wall beams. Pilgrims called themselves "Saints" and referred to everyone else as "Strangers," and even though the Saints were outnumbered, they dominated the *Mayflower*. And this sallow-faced Saint loathed her. He really carried the division between the everyday world and the Pilgrims to the extreme, and he would never let her forget it!

Well, so be it. She didn't want to associate with the Saints any more than they wanted to be with her. But she couldn't help worrying. She had to find a niche for herself, and so far she hadn't seen one friendly face. What if no one took her in when she arrived in the New World? What would she do? Would she have to go back to England on the *Mayflower*'s return voyage? Never!

Chapter
Two

MERRIE lurched along the dark, narrow gangway, her heart pounding. How she dreaded to meet the passengers face-to-face and be reviled as the "stowaway." And the stifling odors made her gag. She held her fur collar to her nose to shut them out.

Stepping into the black damp living quarters, Merrie blinked, trying to accustom her eyes to the gloom. Several women bent over a charcoal brazier, stirring boiling soup. One hollow-cheeked woman glanced up when Merrie's shadow fell across her cooking space. "Who might you be?" she asked, her eyes narrowing.

"I-I'm Merrie Courtland," she answered, and although her voice was small, a certain calm had settled over her. Now that she'd been discovered, the worst was over. She glanced about in the dim corners. A few women lay on pallets while a group of men huddled in quiet conversation. "Master William Brewster sent me," Merrie said.

"Oh?" the older woman looked up. Her gray dress with a small gray cape over it matched her slate-gray hair. "I'm Mary Brewster, William Brewster's wife." She indicated the woman next to her. "This is Elizabeth Hopkins."

"Hello," Merrie said, unable to force a smile, but there were no answering smiles, anyway. In fact, Mistress Hopkins frowned at her, but perhaps it was because she was uncomfortable. It looked as if her baby were due any day.

"I'm to sleep in bunk eighteen," Merrie said, hesitating. "I hid in the longboat." Then she added quickly, "I'm to help with — with the cooking and mending."

Mary Brewster, a lean, practical woman, said matter-of-factly, "You can cut up onions for the soup."

Distastefully, Merrie looked around. She didn't know how to cook, and what was more, she didn't want to learn. But despite the watery appearance of the pea soup, it looked and smelled delicious after her diet of apples. She supposed if she wanted to eat she'd have to slice onions.

"The onions are in a sack by the water kegs," Mistress Brewster said, handing her a knife.

Bending to scoop up some onions, Merrie caught a glimpse of herself in the stagnant drinking water and stopped dead-still. She touched her too-thin face. Her brown eyes were rimmed with black circles, and her cheek hollows were even more sunken. Her hand strayed to her blond hair, fingering the limp strands that were as disheveled as a dust mop.

Disheartened, she took a handful of onions and began peeling. She was so tired, and her eyes watered, not so much from the strong onions as from being bone-weary.

"Not like that!" Elizabeth Hopkins said, snatching the onion from Merrie's hand. "You're peeling half the onion away!" She held the onion in one veined hand, deftly wielding the knife with quick, sure strokes.

"I-I see," said Merrie, tears blinding her. She hated this job — hated the smell, and hated these dreary women. She yearned to go back to her small boat and pull the canvas over her head.

Suddenly a young freckle-faced girl skipped over to Mistress Hopkins. "Mama," she chirped, "Resolved wants me to play leapfrog on deck. Can I?" The girl, whose eyes were slightly slanted, looked appealingly at her mother.

"No, Constanta," Mistress Hopkins said, "it's not proper for a young lady."

Merrie gazed sadly at the little girl, and wondered why she couldn't run and play.

"Constanta," her mother said, "this is your new bedmate."

Constanta spun around, dark skirts flying, and noticed Merrie for the first time. "But I have my own bed," she said firmly.

"Hush, child," Mistress Hopkins said. "You're to share your bed!" Elizabeth Hopkins's lips pressed together in a straight line. "Show Merrie the way." She took the pan from Merrie. "I'll finish the onions." She frowned, staring at the strange, unevenly shaped onions, and added, "What's left of them."

Take the onions, Merrie thought, and good riddance! She hadn't asked for the job in the first place.

Constanta brushed back wisps of brown hair that escaped from her snug purple bonnet fringed with white edges. "This way," she said, stepping swiftly over the legs and feet of the passengers who sprawled in the crowded aisle.

Merrie looked at the small damp mattress and wondered how the two of them would be able to sleep in such a tiny space, but she didn't dwell on it. Instead, she crawled across the straw-filled pallet, wanting only to sleep. Flinging an arm over her eyes, she gave in to the roll and pitch of the ship. It felt as if a giant's hand were violently rocking a cradle.

For the next three weeks Merrie spent as much time on deck as possible. Every day was an eternity, and Captain Jones assured them they had at least another month at sea. Could she stand it? It was no fun coming to meals and having the Saints ignore her, or joining a group of playing children and having their game abruptly cease. Now that she no longer had to hide, and since she wasn't invited to be part of the Pilgrims except to cook, mend, and watch the Hopkins's younger children, she had time to wander the top deck and lower decks of the *Mayflower*. She paced from the quarterdeck and upper decks to the main quarters, the galley, and the cargo holds.

All kinds of household items were stored below — pots of iron, brass and copper frying pans, spits, mortars and pestles, lanterns, lamps, hand-looms, sconces, and snuffers. Wooden and pewter plates, mugs, cutlery, hourglasses, sundials, and all the tools needed for planting and building were packed to the rafters. She peered into Captain Christopher Jones's large cabin, which he'd turned over to twenty of the more important Pilgrims. Their sleeping area was larger than the pallets below deck, but Merrie didn't care. She only wanted to get to the New World.

One evening Merrie carried her supper to the upper deck. She was glad today was a Meat Day, although she was as heartily sick of salted pork or "salt horse" as she was of dried fish. Squeezing a bit of lemon juice into her mouth, she puckered up her lips at the sour taste, but to stay healthy, she knew she had to have lemon and dried fruit. She breathed deeply of the sweetly pungent smell of the ship. The *Mayflower* had once been a wine ship, and over the years the leaking wine vats had saturated her timbers.

As Merrie watched the green and purple waters swell and dip, she glimpsed John Alden, the cooper, or barrel maker. She often saw him on deck checking the water barrels, wine barrels, and hogsheads of beer for leaks. When he straightened from examining a wine vat, he was joined by Priscilla Mullins. The two of them were spending more and more time together, Merrie noted. Eighteen-year-old Priscilla was only a few years older than Merrie. Even though John and Priscilla were Strangers as was Merrie herself, they seemed to be accepted by the Saints. Other Strangers, such as Miles Standish and his wife, Rose, were accepted, too, plus all the common people, the tanners, weavers, and shopkeepers who hoped to build a better life for themselves. Were they tolerated by the Saints because they would be contributing members of the colony? Well, she wanted a better life, too, and just because she didn't have a skill didn't mean she couldn't be useful!

Oh, Merrie thought, I don't know what goes on in the heads of the Pilgrims, and furthermore I don't care. I'm tired of being lonely, and tired of the Saints! I just want to land and face whatever the New World has to offer! She wondered how the settlers of Virginia, the course the compass was set for, would receive a boatload of Saints.

The brisk west breeze blew Merrie's long

hair around her face, and she absentmindedly pushed it back as she watched the twilight's pink glow shimmering on the horizon. Then she shoved her hands in her dress pockets and hunched her shoulders against the ache in her heart. She was overwhelmed with such a deep despair of loneliness. Wouldn't she ever be accepted?

Suddenly a Pilgrim scrambled from the hold up onto the deck, choking and clawing at her throat. Fear, stark and vivid, glittered in her eyes as she staggered to the rail.

For a moment Merrie froze. Then the woman's terrifying gasps threw her into action. She dashed to the woman's side and slapped her on the back. The poor woman, sides heaving and tears coursing down her cheeks, clutched desperately at the railing. Her round face was red, turning blue. Frantic, Merrie continued to pound her back, heedless of the gathering crowd. Bending the woman almost double over the ship's rail, she continued to hit her back. At last a morsel of meat flew from the woman's mouth.

Almost at once the woman stopped her racking breaths and sucked the refreshing air in to fill her lungs. She sank to the deck. Merrie breathed a sigh of relief and leaned down, asking, "Are you all right?"

"Water," the woman rasped. "Water."

Merrie turned quickly to fetch a tankard of water, but a young man brushed past her, already holding a mug. He tipped the rim to the woman's pale lips. A stout man rushed to her side, ignoring the group of wide-eyed men, women, and children who had crowded nearer.

Then Doctor Fuller knelt beside the woman, examining her throat. "Mistress Sedgewick, we wondered why you jumped up and ran from the table. Here," he said soothingly, "let me swab your throat with oil." He glanced up. "Zachariah, fetch my case, will you?"

"Yes, sir," the young man answered quickly. He was a tall dark boy whom Merrie hadn't seen before. He turned abruptly, almost bumping into Merrie. He stopped in surprise and for a moment their eyes met. Merrie, embarrassed, looked down, and he hurried past.

"Is Patience all right, Doctor?" the stout man asked anxiously.

"Your wife will be fine, Daniel."

Daniel took his wife's hand, feverishly rubbing it. "Patience, what happened?"

The woman smiled ruefully, and her plain face lit up. "I'm afraid a piece of pork lodged in my throat." Her gray eyes strayed to Merrie. "If it hadn't been for this young girl, I would have choked to death."

The man grabbed Merrie's hand and shook it. "Thank you, Merrie Courtland, thank you. I'm Daniel Sedgewick, and if there's anything I can do for you, just let me know."

Merrie wasn't surprised that he knew her name. Everyone knew who the stowaway girl was. "I was glad to help," she murmured, but

Mr. Sedgewick wasn't listening. His attention was on his wife.

The young man called Zachariah handed the doctor his case and squatted down beside him. After a long swallow of water, the woman, with the help of her husband, rose unsteadily to her feet.

Oliver Loomis sidled up beside Merrie and sneered, "Don't think you're anything special, Mistress Courtland. I've been observing your willful ways!" His thin lips became thinner. "You're a stowaway who has stolen our food and a place to sleep!"

She flushed under his penetrating stare. His pale cold eyes, the color of rock salt, seemed to burn through her. It was as if they riveted her to the spot.

Just then Daniel led his wife down to the hold and called over his shoulder, "Thank you again, Mistress Merrie." Then he — and Oliver Loomis — disappeared below along with the others.

A cold knot formed in Merrie's stomach. Perhaps she should have stayed in England. Even though she had saved Patience Sedgewick's life, things were the same as ever, only worse. Daniel Sedgewick's offer of help was a hollow one, and she could never forget the look of loathing on Master Loomis's face. A tremor slid over her. That man wouldn't leave her alone until he carried out his threat — and if she were forced to leave the colony, it would be the same as a death sentence!

Chapter Three

"MERRIE, come here a moment," Elizabeth Hopkins's shrill voice reverberated throughout the lower deck.

Merrie, lying in bed, jumped up and jammed her stockinged feet into her slippers. Was it time for Elizabeth's baby? Or was it another job she wanted done?

The ship pitched, causing Merrie to falter as she hurried to Mistress Hopkins's side. She'd been at sea seven weeks and still couldn't get used to being ordered about and being crowded in with so many people day and night. Oh, for some privacy!

Elizabeth Hopkins sat brushing her young son Damaris's long hair. But it didn't do much good, Merrie thought. His face was grimy, and there were traces of yesterday's pea soup dribbled on his vest.

But after sleeping in her clothes for so long and not being able to bathe, she was as dirty as Damaris and her long curly hair was even more tangled. She did try to wash her face, but using the salt water hauled up to scrub the decks didn't do much good. She'd trade anything for a hot freshwater bath.

"Merrie, will you go down to the hold and help Master Gaines catch six chickens that got loose?" Elizabeth Hopkins shifted uncomfortably.

"You mean someone opened the cages?" Merrie asked incredulously.

"Yes, one of the sailors." Elizabeth shook her head in disgust. "Anything to annoy us! Now, hurry along. We need chickens if we're going to have chicken stew."

"Yes, Mistress Hopkins," Merrie said reluctantly. Passing Damaris, she playfully tweaked his nose and was rewarded with a gap-toothed grin. If she wasn't accepted by the adults, she thought, at least the children had grown to like her.

In the hold, Merrie hurried along the dark passage, afraid of seeing a rat. The dampness penetrated her bones, and the smell of the sloshing bilge water nauseated her.

A squawk startled her, and a chicken flew across her path. Diving for the bird, Merrie sprawled flat on the wet slimy floor, grasping only two white tail feathers in her hand. "Drat," she muttered, slowly picking herself up and futilely brushing off her soiled dress.

Clucking frantically, the chicken flew behind several tubs and buckets. Merrie glared about the gloomy hold. Where was that stupid chicken? She was going to catch it if it was the last thing she did!

Scrambling over baskets and pails, she suddenly came face-to-face with Zachariah Gaines.

"Whoa!" he said. "Slow down, mistress!" He cocked a black bushy brow at her. "Did they send you down here to help me?" He leaned against the wire mesh cage containing five of the six chickens and surveyed her.

"Yes," she answered quickly, "and if we hurry, we can catch the last one. It flew over there, but I couldn't get my hands on it."

He eyed her dirt-streaked dress and smudged face. A faint, mocking smile touched his lips. "You'd better let me handle this, 'stowaway girl,'" he said.

His patronizing tone infuriated her, and she rolled up her sleeves. "I'll catch it myself!" she said, thrusting out her chin. She glanced over her shoulder and said curtly, "And don't call me 'stowaway girl'!"

His low chuckle made her cheeks flame. Soon, however, she forgot him as she became intent on catching the elusive chicken.

She crept silently among the stored blankets and rugs. Glimpsing the chicken, she grabbed for a leg, caught the shrieking bird, and triumphantly thrust it into the cage.

There! That should show this mocking fellow!

"You know, I admire your quick thinking," he said. "You saved Patience Sedgewick's life."

Surprised by his words, she didn't know how to respond.

"Everyone is grateful," he went on solemnly.

"So grateful they hurried to get away from me again," she replied bitterly.

He laughed, but this time it was a low, pleasant sound that seemed to rumble up from his chest. "They wanted to get out of the cold and back to their suppers. Can you blame them?" She noticed the gleam of his black eyes and the way he watched her every move. Embarrassed, she attempted to smooth back her hair, but, like a bramble bush, it stubbornly sprang back on her forehead.

Abruptly he said, "Let's get out of this smelly place." Mutely she followed him through the passageway and up the stairs into the fresh salt air.

Reaching the deck, she turned to him, pleased that he'd spoken civilly to her, and asked, "Are you Doctor Fuller's assistant?"

He nodded. "Since William Butten, his servant, died, I've been helping with the dysentery cases below. It's bad down there." He paused, and she noticed that his dull brown breeches and leather jerkin looked good on his lean figure. His black curls ringed his head like a halo of black feathers. "I can see why you spend so much time on deck."

She lifted her brows at his knowledge of her daily routine. He held out his hand. "I'm Zachariah Gaines. And you're the 'stowaway girl,' right?" A small smile flickered across his face.

She stiffened and withdrew her hand. "I'm Merrie Courtland," she retorted defiantly.

"You're a stowaway!" he repeated.

"I had no choice!" she answered. Zachariah was just like everyone else. He might be civil, but he also divided the world into who was right and who was wrong! She leaned over the rail, watching the glassy sea. Finally she spoke. "I'm worried about Elizabeth Hopkins," she said. "Since you're the doctor's assistant, perhaps you could look in on her."

"I'm sorry," he said dryly, his good manners returning, "but my doctoring skills are limited to carrying out Doctor Fuller's orders." He looked at her crestfallen face. "I'll tell him, though. Anyway, no more doctoring for me. When we land, I'll set up a fur trading business and export beaver pelts to England."

She stared at him. Somehow his answer disappointed her. He, like Jeremiah, was just another merchant, she thought. She detested merchants!

"The French can't have the only monopoly on the fur trade," Zachariah went on easily. "The Saints owe Thomas Weston and his company, The Merchant Adventurers, a great deal of money. We agreed to send out lumber and furs back to England for the next seven years. By that time I'll be twenty-five and experienced enough to set up my own business."

She didn't really want to hear about his fur trade ventures. He was such a dashing, handsome young man. Why couldn't he be a doctor like Samuel Fuller?

The sudden pitch and roll of the ship caught her by surprise, and she tumbled forward into his arms. Zachariah calmly braced himself before setting her back on her feet.

Merrie, feeling hot blood rush to her cheeks, hastily moved back an arm's length. She turned quickly and stared at the greenish-black sky and the now roiling ocean. A splinter of lightning creased the black clouds. "I hope we don't have another storm," she said lamely.

He smiled grimly. "You don't wish it half as much as I do!" He pushed back a lock of thick dark hair.

"What a stench below! In the last storm the buckets filled faster than they could be emptied. I couldn't get from one person to the next without falling at least once. But — you seem to have your sea legs, Mistress Courtland."

She welcomed his teasing tone, and smiled, and her brown eyes twinkled. Zachariah was friendlier than she had first thought. "Probably," she said, smiling appealingly, "because I keep myself occupied by calming the younger children."

Thunder rumbled, and lightning speared the sky. "We'd better get below, before the storm really hits," Zachariah said. "The doctor probably needs me."

A clap of thunder split the air, and the *Mayflower* dipped sharply. The ocean's waves, crested with whitecaps, churned higher and higher. Merrie hoped Elizabeth Hopkins's baby wouldn't come in this storm.

"Zack!" Doctor Fuller shouted. "Come down here!"

"Coming," he called, touching her elbow. "Let's get below, Mistress Courtland."

"You go ahead," she urged. "I want to stay and watch the storm." Tasting the salt spray that misted across her face, she waved at him.

"Be careful, then!" His teeth flashed, and he was gone. She turned back to the wind and sea, musing about Zachariah's self-confidence and his off-again, on-again disapproval of the "stowaway girl." Although it upset her, still and all there was something about this Pilgrim youth that stirred unfamiliar feelings within her.

Merrie turned her face back into the freezing gale. She knew she should go below, but she had to stay a minute longer to feel the strength of the churning ocean and the snapping sails.

The storm was blowing toward full fury

now, and foaming waves cascaded over the deck. The ship plunged down into the hollow of the giant ocean, then fought her way up the other side of the trough of water. Frightened and exhilarated at the same time, Merrie clutched the railing until her knuckles whitened and watched as Luke and three crewmen secured the cannon and bolted tight the portholes. Others ran up the shrouds to furl the sails, struggling to lash them against the tearing wind. Merrie wondered if the staunch little ship would be able to take such a beating.

Then Luke spied Merrie. "Merrie Courtland! Get below!" he bellowed.

Merrie didn't want another confrontation with Luke Bosworth. Drenched in rain and flying spray, she dutifully stumbled and slipped her way toward the hatch. The glaring sailor met her there and flung it open. "Fool girl," he grumbled, his words almost lost on the tearing wind.

Soaked to the skin, Merrie hurried below, where the Pilgrims huddled together. The westerly gale pounded the ship like a giant sledgehammer. Icy water poured in through the seams, further drenching Merrie's already sodden dress.

For hours the tiny ship battled fierce crosswinds. Mutterings of fear and alarm filled the hold.

The storm raged all the next day, mercilessly battering the ship. Merrie couldn't stop her teeth from chattering. She shivered miserably in her wet heavy wool dress.

Trying to distract Damaris, the five-year-old son of Elizabeth and Stephen Hopkins, Merrie tickled his ears with a feather, but he wouldn't stop crying. Worriedly she glanced at Elizabeth Hopkins, who lay in her bunk, wretchedly groaning with every creak of the ship.

Suddenly a boom like a cannon shot was heard above the howling winds, and the ship listed dangerously to one side. Water gushed over Merrie, drenching her hair, her face, and her dress, right down to her petticoats.

William Bradford patted the arm of his weeping young wife and swiftly hastened topside.

When he returned, his face was ashen. "The main beam amidship has snapped!" he said grimly. "The deck is splintered."

Cries and moans rose to the rafters. Despairingly Merrie clasped Damaris tighter. How she despised this ship! Then a quavery voice rose in a psalm, above all the rest. Soon others joined in:

"Yea though I walk in dale of deadly shade
I fear no ill; for with me thou wilt be.
Thy rod, thy staff, they comfort me.
Before me, thou hast made ready a table.
In their presence that my distressers be."

The ship lurched downward sickeningly. Was this the end? Merrie wondered.

Chapter Four

ANOTHER deluge of icy ocean water cascaded over Merrie, but suddenly, after two days of the storm, she didn't care. She couldn't comprehend this new danger. Her bones ached, and so did her head. She held her stomach, which heaved along with the ship. She felt sick. All at once she jumped off her pallet and reached for the wooden bucket. The retching fit left her weaker than ever. She retched and retched until, sinking to the wet deck, she sat in a corner with her chin resting on her knees. Miserably she tried to shut out the screaming wind while her wet skirts clung to her like a second skin, chilling her to the bone. She wondered vaguely what would happen to them now that the main beam had snapped. Would the ship be cut in two? Already the battered ship wallowed in the overpowering waves. Without a mainmast they would sink.

John Carver, the acknowledged leader of the Pilgrims, looked sharply at William Bradford and William Brewster. "We must make a quick decision," he said, his face grim and drawn. "Either we turn back or we go forward." Although only in his forties, Master Carver's face was heavily lined, and silver sprinkled his brown hair.

Unnoticed where she huddled, Merrie watched as the three men put their heads together. They were the elected Elders, or rulers, of the congregation and made all the decisions, not only for the group from Leiden but from London as well. Most of the Londoners were Strangers, many belonging to the Church of England, and they resented the Pilgrims taking charge. But since the Saints had financed the voyage, there wasn't much they could do about it.

"Let's turn back," Edward Winslow said, another Elder who had joined them.

"I think we should go back to England, too," William Brewster said reluctantly. "If we continue to sail west, we'll never see a ship."

William Bradford nodded his head, agreeing with Brewster. And why wouldn't he, thought Merrie. After all, he'd lived with the Brewsters in Leiden and was like their adopted son. "I'll ask Captain Jones to turn her around."

Turn back to England? After all this time at sea? They couldn't!

The men lowered their voices, and Merrie

no longer strained to hear. What was the use? Back to England! The image of Jeremiah loomed before her.

Suddenly, Moses Fletcher, the ship's carpenter, pushed his way forward. "I have a jack-screw here in the hold," he stated matter-of-factly. "We can straighten the mainmast back in place and secure it with an iron hoop."

The leaders glanced at one another.

All at once William Bradford leaped to his feet, slapping Moses on the back. "You're right! It could work!"

"What are we waiting for?" Edward Winslow asked, a smile spreading across his face. "The mast will be as sturdy as before!"

John Carver scrambled up the steps, shouting happily, "I'll see what Captain Jones has to say."

A jack! The simple tool Merrie had glimpsed in the hold. It was supposed to be used for building houses, but now it could save their lives!

After hours of work the men successfully wedged the mast back in place. The Pilgrims had labored alongside the sailors to secure it and even had manned the pumps to pump out the standing waist-deep water in the hold. Exhausted as she was, Merrie felt overwhelming relief. They were sailing west to the New World after all!

In the next week the sea calmed, the sun shone brilliantly, and the hatches were flung open. Merrie helped Patience Sedgewick lug the soggy bedding topside and spread the wet blankets on the decks to dry.

Others walked the deck or just leaned over the rail breathing in the fresh salt air. Children skipped rope, tossed a ball back and forth, or chased the two dogs around the deck.

Merrie had cooked all day. How good it would be to taste a hot meal tonight, for during any wind it was forbidden to use the charcoal braziers; a single spark could set the ship afire. Constanta had even helped her stir the stew. Since being bedmates, Constanta wanted to be at Merrie's side more and more. Merrie was pleased, too, that the Hopkins family had grudgingly accepted her, although Master Stephen Hopkins growled at her every time she came near. He was always in a bad mood, and Merrie avoided him as much as possible. But today she wouldn't let anything bother her. She leaned back against a water cask, letting the sun's rays sink into her frozen bones.

"Hello, Merrie Courtland," came a gruff voice with a touch of humor underneath. Luke, his foot perched on the water barrel, looked down at her.

She sat up straight. "Hello," she said, tentatively, wondering why, after all these weeks, Luke was speaking to her.

His red curls turned to copper flame in the sunlight, and his grin warmed her more than the sun. "I see you survived the storm," he said lightly.

"And you survived, too," she answered banteringly.

"That I did," he announced proudly, "but it wasn't easy climbing that mizzenmast!"

"Oh, no," she said, aghast. "You climbed a mast in that wind?"

"I'll tell you the wind almost tore me loose a time or two, but it wasn't as bad as the time I sailed around Cape Horn." He gave her a broad wink. "Magellan didn't name the tip of South America the 'Cape of Storms' for nothing!" His face sobered. "One of my shipmates was washed overboard, and another had a leg crushed by a flying boom." Gazing at her, Luke smiled again, light spreading over his round face as he hitched up his cutoff trousers. "But look at us — safe and sound as a babe in a cradle!" His eyes danced when he looked at her. "You know, I've been wanting to tell you I thought you were fine, saving that Pilgrim woman's life."

"Why, thank you, Luke Bosworth." So that's why he'd changed. Quite a different attitude from the day he'd pulled her out of her hiding place and forced her to confront the captain.

"You're a pretty girl, Merrie Courtland," he said admiringly. "The salt spray agrees with you. Your hair is like a golden cloud."

Laughing, Merrie touched her hair which was tumbling over her shoulders. "It will take me a week to brush out the tangles. If we ever land, I'll wash it over and over again. When do you think we'll see Virginia?"

"Well," he said, sticking his thumbs beneath his arms to pace back and forth with the rolling gait of a seaman, "I'd say we'll be on the Atlantic at least a fortnight."

"Two more weeks?" she echoed in disbelief.

"Maybe three," Luke replied, with a shrug. "But you notice the waters are changing from blue to a greenish color, which means land isn't too far away."

"I can't wait to set my feet on good firm soil," she said. "I'm tired of walking sideways like a crab, trying to keep my balance. I'm tired of dirty looks, sickness, and wormy food."

Luke chuckled and shook his head. "If you'd watch sailors eat hardtack, you'd learn something. Just knock your biscuit on the table, and the weevils will scuttle out real fast. I've seen you try to pick the little devils out by hand, and that takes forever!" He sat down beside her. "But tell me, Mistress Courtland, where will you stay when we drop anchor?"

She lowered her thick lashes, not wanting to meet his eyes. How could she admit she didn't have a place? "I-I don't know just yet," she answered in a low voice.

"You can always sail back on the *Mayflower*'s return voyage," he said jauntily. "We'll be heading back as soon as we unload the Saints." He emphasized the last word in a mocking tone. "You don't belong with them, Mistress Courtland."

"And return to Jeremiah Farmingham? No thanks." The last thing she wanted was Luke's pity. "I'll find a home," she said more confidently than she felt. "Don't worry about me, Luke."

He grinned. "You're a spunky girl," he said, admiration in his blue eyes. "You must have hated London to run away."

"No," she said thoughtfully, "I had a good life there. But I couldn't face marrying an old man, could I?"

Luke grinned, taking off the green knit cap that matched his knit stockings, and tucking it in his leather belt. "Guess not."

She enjoyed sitting here with Luke. He was friendly, and she longed to have a friend.

All at once an explosion reverberated throughout the ship.

Startled, Merrie glanced quickly at the mainsail but saw that everything abovedeck was serene and that the sails were unfurled in their full glory. Her pulse quickened. "What was that?" she exclaimed, shooting Luke a frightened look.

A worried frown creased his forehead. "I don't know, but I aim to find out." He grabbed her hand. "It came from below!"

Passengers and sailors rushed past them to get to the hold where the gunpowder kegs were stored. When Merrie and Luke pushed their way in, Miles Standish, his veins bulging on his forehead, was glaring at plump Francis Billington. The fourteen-year-old boy was holding a squib, a small noisy firecracker, and a musket taller than he was.

"You what?" roared Captain Standish.

"I-I shot off the musket." His lips trembled.

Captain Standish thundered, "You could have blown up the whole ship!" He mopped his forehead with a large handkerchief. "Meddling brat! You're always into something!"

Mr. Billington rushed forward, putting his arm around his son. "No need to shout at Francis!" he said stiffly.

"Someone has to!" Miles Standish retorted furiously. "Why don't you watch him?"

"Here, here, Miles," John Carver said calmly. "No need to shout."

"What would you do, John?" Miles snatched the musket from Francis's hands.

"I'll discipline my own son!" Master Billington said angrily.

"Ha!" Standish growled. "And what will you do, slap his hands?"

Master Billington snarled, "You Saints think you can order everyone around! Well, you're in for a surprise once we land!" Then he was gone.

Merrie and Luke left, too. Luke laughed off the incident, but she couldn't. The bitter antagonism between Saints and Strangers became sharper and more biting every day. How could they live together if they were constantly at one another's throats?

Chapter Five

BLUSTERING November arrived, and still no land appeared. Would they ever see good solid earth again, Merrie wondered as she sat on deck mending her cloak.

Merrie glanced up as a sailor reversed the half-hour sandglass and struck a bell that hung from a beam on the poop deck. Putting aside her mended cloak, she opened the book she'd borrowed from William Brewster's library. He'd brought along over two hundred books and willingly lent them to anyone interested. Merrie was delighted, for she'd read and reread her myth books. She had to admit, though, that her present book, John Milton's *Paradise Lost*, was much more difficult and not nearly so interesting as the myth of Apollo.

"Good morning, Mistress Courtland," Susanna White said, walking by with Dorothy Bradford.

Merrie closed her book and smiled. "Good morning, Mistress White." She felt a warm glow at being spoken to. Since she had saved Patience Sedgewick's life, more and more of the Pilgrims spoke to her.

Mistress White, Dr. Fuller's sister, smiled in return, and walked by. As with Elizabeth Hopkins, her baby was due any day, too. Dorothy Bradford glanced at Merrie, nodding distractedly. How frail and delicate William Bradford's wife appeared. She was only twenty-three but looked ten years older. Merrie felt a lump in her throat when she glimpsed the pain in Dorothy's eyes, especially when Dorothy watched five-year-old Resolved White hug his mother. No doubt she was remembering her own five-year-old son, left behind because the voyage would be too hard on the weak little boy. Dorothy grieved openly, and these days her husband had very little time to comfort her.

After taking a turn around the deck, the two women disappeared, but Merrie didn't reopen her book. She was weary of the sea. She had worked hard trying not to be a burden, but now she was scared. Although they'd sight land any day, still no one had offered her a place to stay. Perhaps, like the seven indentured servants on board, she could attach herself to a household. But that thought was more terrifying than returning to England. She didn't want to be bound to a family for seven years. She had come too far, gone through too much, to give up her freedom. Maybe if she became a Saint, she mused, and worshipped as they did, they'd welcome her. She had no quarrel with their idea of a pure and simple church — no candles, incense, or altars — but she did find their long hours of prayer and their Sunday services too long and too austere. They didn't even allow an organ, calling it the "devil's bagpipes." She sighed. Their ways were not her ways.

Suddenly, Zachariah dashed past her. "Merrie," he shouted. "Hurry! Elizabeth Hopkins wants you!"

Her throat closed. Was the baby coming? Numbly she got to her feet. What could she do? She was afraid even to hold a baby, much less help deliver one!

But when she came into the dark hold, Dr. Fuller handed her a tiny wrapped bundle. "It's a boy," he said, turning back to Elizabeth.

Gingerly, Merrie lifted the baby, looking down at his shriveled red face. How natural it felt to hold a squirming infant.

"Merrie, will you watch Damaris and Constanta?" Elizabeth weakly asked.

She looked into Elizabeth's weary eyes. "Of course," she answered softly. "You know I will." How good it felt to be of some use and not to be resented as she'd been a few weeks ago.

Stephen Hopkins stepped forward, taking

the baby from Merrie. "Oceanus," he said proudly. "That's my son's name. Oceanus Hopkins!"

The next morning she resumed her place on deck and again picked up her mending. As she stitched she thought of yesterday and Oceanus's marvelous birth. What a darling ugly baby, she thought, smiling to herself. She was glad Elizabeth was doing fine, too. The breeze ruffled Merrie's hair, and she let it fly. Her long hair felt good since Constanta had brushed and brushed it last night. Most of the tangles were out, but her hair still hung lank. The first thing she'd do when they reached land was to give it a good scrubbing. They should soon sight land — Captain Jones had even put on an additional watch.

"Good morning, 'stowaway girl,'" Zachariah called, weaving his way through the coils of ropes and kegs, and moving rapidly toward her.

She glared at him, irked at being called a stowaway. "I'm Merrie Courtland," she replied firmly, but forgave him when he grinned at her so engagingly.

"Merrie," he said easily, "since you have your needle and thread handy, would you do me a favor?" A red shirt was draped over his arm, and his dark face seemed lit by an inner light.

"Yes, Zachariah?" she responded, knowing very well what he wanted. "Some mending, perhaps?" She found it impossible not to return his disarming smile.

"Call me Zack."

"Very well, Zack," she repeated, enjoying the pleasing sound.

He handed her his shirt. "When I pumped out the bilge water, the undersleeve split." He cocked his head. "Would you mind?"

She laughed. "If you trust me. My stitches aren't the smallest or neatest."

"I don't care." He hunkered down alongside, pushing back his black wide-brimmed hat. "You know, Merrie," he said quietly, "you were a big help yesterday with the Hopkins family."

A warm pink glow touched her cheeks. Perhaps he thought she could be useful after all, even if he did refer to her as "stowaway girl."

As she stitched, she stole a glance at his face. It was tinged with an amused expression as he observed her. His sparkling ebony eyes, fringed with long dark lashes, were set off by the thickest, blackest brows she'd ever seen. "Zack," she began hesitantly, "are you alone on this voyage?"

"I'm alone," he echoed. "But I wasn't supposed to be." For a moment his faint smile held a touch of sadness. "You see, I lived in London until I was five. When my parents died within a month of each other, my maiden aunt took me in. Being part of the Separatist group, we went to Holland to escape King

James. I was only six when we arrived in Leiden. Aunt Mary worked as a weaver, and I helped card wool. Later, like Bradford, I became a weaver." He paused, and his lips tightened, "A vocation I don't plan to continue!"

"I know," she responded, her eyes dancing. "You'll be a trapper and export furs."

He lifted his dark brows. "Ah, you remembered." He ran his fingers through his thick curly hair. "But even if I don't miss my loom, I do miss Leiden." He glanced at her. "The Dutch were a fun-loving people. Too fun-loving for the Saints. After twelve years of living in Holland, the Saints felt their children were becoming corrupt. The Dutch," he went on, tossing his head and laughing, "didn't believe in listening to a five-hour sermon Sunday morning and a four-hour one in the afternoon." He shook his head, still smiling. "After the Dutch attended church, they hurried off to ice-skate or play with their children. I grew up with Dutch customs, Dutch ideas, and the Dutch language. My aunt, along with other Pilgrims, decided to leave Leiden before we inherited their evil ways!" He grinned at her, his lips parting to display dazzling white teeth. "Maybe I'm already infected."

"But your aunt didn't sail with you?" Merrie questioned, puzzled.

"Well, Aunt Mary started out with me. You see, the Leiden group sailed on the

Speedwell, the ship that accompanied the *Mayflower*."

"Oh, yes," she said, inspecting the stitches. "I heard the *Speedwell* was so leaky it had to turn back." Satisfied with her sewing, she handed Zack his shirt.

"Thanks," he said, continuing his explanation. "Since the *Mayflower* was already filled to capacity, not everyone could squeeze aboard. Besides, quite a few had had enough of ocean travel, including my aunt. She decided to stay on the *Speedwell* and return to London. I'll miss her." His tone softened. "She was good to me, even if she was strict."

"Who — who will you be staying with?" she ventured.

"Miles Standish and his wife, Rose." Zack chuckled. "If Miles's energy and temper don't drive me crazy. The captain has taken a liking to me and wants my help in training his men. He said I can handle a musket almost better than himself."

"Since you're an expert, will you give me a lesson?" she asked. "I'd like to learn to fire a musket."

"You?" An amused look flickered across Zack's lean face. "You'd better stick to cooking and — " he examined the red shirt-sleeve " — your sewing."

A slight frown creased her forehead. After surviving this voyage she felt she could do anything. But she didn't argue with him. She couldn't stand to have him laugh at her again. Somehow his approval meant a great deal to her.

He continued easily, "I won't be staying with Miles long. As soon as possible I'll build my own cabin. All I'll need is furniture — " he looked at her appraisingly " — and a wife."

She couldn't meet his steady scrutiny. Surely he didn't mean her. Disquieting ideas raced through her mind. No, no, she hastily assured herself. Zack was far too sensible to get involved with a "stowaway girl." Bewildered at such strange thoughts, she jumped up, exclaiming, "Oh, look at the sandglass. I promised I'd watch Oceanus."

His bold stare disconcerted her, and she hastily gathered up her cloak. She didn't want him to question her about her own future.

Hurrying away, she glanced back, ready with a smile and a wave, but her hand froze in midair when she saw Oliver Loomis intensely talking to Zack. Suddenly the tall man pointed a bony finger in her direction. Zack, arms folded, nodded his head thoughtfully. What had Master Loomis said to him? Oliver Loomis pounded his fist against his palm, to make a point, then glared at her. Merrie shuddered at his glittering black look of fury. Her blood began to pound in her temples, and she spun about, unable to dash down the steps and into the hold fast enough.

Chapter Six

THE next week Merrie was kept busy with Elizabeth and her new baby, but every time she thought of Oliver Loomis, a chill crept over her. Several times she dodged behind a mast or ran to the opposite railing to avoid facing him. On the morning of November 8th, Merrie gazed out over the heaving ocean, numb with cold. But the freezing wind was better than listening to families discuss their landing plans and the kind of cabins they'd build.

If she were back in England, Father might be taking her to Coventry Square for a new frock, all ribbons and ruffles. She rubbed her forehead. No, no, she thought. She didn't want a new dress. She wanted to tell him how much she loved him, how much she needed him. But a worrying thought crept into her mind. Even though Father had pampered her, he had always held her at arm's length, never hugging her, never telling her that he loved her. Was it her fault, she wondered. Was she too self-centered?

Stern Matilda had once warned her to set a few goals . . . to aim for something in life. Well, their housekeeper would be proud of her. Merrie had done nothing but think about her future since she'd stowed away. She smiled grimly. She'd even learned how to peel an onion. She remembered the night when she'd sneaked aboard amid the loaded crates and kegs, thinking the voyage would be such a lark. It had been anything but fun! She felt so alone, so empty inside. No one wanted her. Tears welled up, and even when she wiped them away, the ocean waves still blurred. Why had she ever come?

"Merrie," a woman's voice called.

Merrie looked up, pushing away her thoughts.

Patience and Daniel Sedgewick stood watching her.

Hastily, Merrie brushed aside her tears. "Yes?" she asked, wondering what they wanted.

Quickly, Patience went to her and placed a hand on her wrist. "Daniel has something to ask you," she said, a small smile around her pressed lips.

Daniel Sedgewick, appearing stern in his dark clothes, approached her, his thin hair blowing about his face. "When we land, Mistress Courtland," he cleared his throat, glancing nervously at his wife, "we — we wondered if you'd like to stay with us?"

Merrie's heart leaped, and she clasped Patience's hand. "Oh, yes, yes, I would," she said. "Do you really mean it?" She wanted to run and hug Master Sedgewick, but something about his stiff posture kept her back.

"I wouldn't be here if it weren't for you, Merrie," Patience said solemnly, her gray eyes steady on Merrie's. Her tight white cap tied under her chin hid her graying hair.

"Then, it's settled," Daniel said briskly. "When our cabin is built, you'll live with us."

Merrie was ecstatic. She'd have a place to stay in the New World after all! Was it possible? And to think of all the time she'd wasted worrying.

"Come, my dear." Daniel took his wife's elbow, gave Merrie a fleeting smile, and turned away.

Merrie hugged herself with delight. She had a place to stay! She wouldn't have to go back to England after all! But when she thought about her new home, some of her elation evaporated. The truth of the matter was that the Sedgewicks were repaying a favor with a favor, and it was obvious they were none too happy about it.

That night as Merrie lay on her pallet, smelling the new scent of land in the air, she resolved to make the Sedgewicks glad they'd given her a home. She'd scrub, clean, cook, and mend for them. Closing her eyes, she at last drifted off to sleep.

Early the next morning, Merrie wrapped

her cloak about her and went up on deck to stand at the ship's rail. She peered into the distance, but it was still too dark to see if land was on the horizon. Would November 9th be the day? The ocean was an emerald-green in the dawn's light, and Merrie watched a dolphin cavort alongside the ship. A breath of wind filled the sails, and a gull wheeled and dipped on the gray morning air. The horizon loomed dark ahead of her. She caught her breath with anticipation. Was it land? She strained to see.

All at once from the crow's nest came a sailor's bellow: "L-a-a-nd HO! La-a-nd ho!"

Merrie's eyes weren't playing tricks on her after all. The dark strip in the distance was land! Her heart raced, and unable to hold back her exuberance, she let out a whoop of joy.

Saints and Strangers eagerly tumbled up on deck, hugging one another at the sight of the long, low shore. It had been sixty-five days since they'd left Plymouth, and tears of relief mingled with tears of joy on the happy faces. Everyone crowded the rail as the *Mayflower* sailed closer and closer to shore.

Merrie couldn't wait to run on firm soil again. A number of Pilgrims were on their knees, thanking God for delivering them safely. William Brewster, taking off his hat, said in a loud, resonant voice that cracked with emotion, "Let's sing Psalm One Hundred in gratitude."

Immediately, the Saints began to sing, their words soaring above the billowing sails.

"Shout to Jehovah, all the earth
        Serve you Jehovah with gladness
Before him come with singing mirth
        Know that Jehovah he God is
It's he that made us, not we
                His folk and sheep of his feeding
O with confession enter ye
        His gates, his courtyards with
                praising.
Confess to him, bless you his name
                Because Jehovah he good is
His mercy ever is the same
                And his faith, unto all ages."

"Let's have everyone's attention!" Captain Jones, holding up a map, shouted when the hymn ended. "According to John Smith's map of 1614, this is Cape Cod. We're several hundred miles north of Virginia!"

"Oh, no," gasped Patience Sedgewick.

"What will we do?" Susanna White asked.

All eyes fastened on John Carver, who quickly examined the map, but he was interrupted by the first mate muscling through. "Drop anchor here," he said roughly. "The crew wants to get rid of everybody and head back to England before the winter storms."

Merrie, remembering the snapped beam, wondered what they'd just been through. But she could understand why the crew wanted to get rid of them and be in control again.

Captain Jones stood listening, arms folded over his wheat-colored long coat. William Brewster glanced at the captain. "We signed a contract! Take us to Virginia," he said firmly.

The captain shrugged, his black flat-brimmed hat shading his face. "If we sail south, it's at least sixty knots."

William Brewster cast a resigned glance at John Carver, who reluctantly nodded.

John Carver leaped up on a small keg. "Good people," he shouted, "we've come this far. Let's be strong. Now we must sail on to our Virginia Company grant. I know how eager you are to touch blessed earth once more, but in a few days we'll be in Virginia, our true destination."

"Aye," growled John Billington. "We need to go on!"

Merrie's stomach knotted. Land was so near. She couldn't bear to sail on!

Mutterings of despair ran through the crowd, particularly among those Saints who would just as soon settle here, out of the reach of King James, whose laws controlled the Virginia Company. The Strangers, however, wanted to sail on.

Captain Jones ordered the sailors to tack and change direction. Merrie's sudden joy of sighting land changed to bitter disappointment as she watched the shoreline recede into the distance.

For several hours, the *Mayflower* plowed

through the foamy waves until the lookout shouted, "Breakers ahead!"

Almost immediately the roaring choppy waters began to buffet the ship, first one way, then the other.

Merrie, thrown to the deck, crawled to a mast. Rising to her feet, she hugged the wooden pole as the ship rocked and pitched. She was certain the bottom would be ripped open.

Luke, after securing the topsail, spied Merrie and rushed over. They stood clutching each other with the mast between them. "We're in Tucker's Terror," he yelled. "Hold tight!"

Her eyes wide with fright, Merrie gazed at Luke. After all the agonizing weeks at sea, were they to be smashed to pieces while still in sight of land? She groaned. "Luke, why couldn't we have anchored at Cape Cod?"

"The Saints are a stubborn lot," Luke said, managing a lopsided grin. "I'm glad I don't have to live with them."

The ship lurched toward the bottom, and Merrie's stomach plummeted, too. She moaned, closing her eyes, feeling Luke's strong hands tighten on hers. No, she thought resolutely, clenching her teeth, she would not die this way! After all they'd suffered, surely they wouldn't sink now.

"We're turning back!" Captain Jones shouted. "Back to Cape Cod. We've got to get out of these dangerous breakers!"

With superb seamanship, the captain was able to turn about and head back to where they'd just sailed.

Open conflict broke out now. The Strangers wanted to be under the protection of the Virginia Company and insisted on going on, even through the breakers! They didn't want the Saints making laws that they would have to live by!

William Brewster, one of the Saint's Elders, and Stephen Hopkins, a Stranger, looked at each other. "We've got a mutiny on our hands," Master Brewster said, grimly looking about at the angry passengers.

"Aye," Stephen Hopkins agreed. "We'd better try to get some order!"

"Let's go below," William Brewster said purposefully, "and set to work! With your writing skills, Master Hopkins, I'm certain we can write some laws that both sides can live by." He motioned for John Carver and several others to follow him.

At dawn the next day the men, looking tired and disheveled, emerged from the hold. William Brewster gathered everyone about him. "The Mayflower Compact is complete!" he said sternly, holding up a parchment and looking over the subdued crowd, "and I promise you the anchor won't be dropped until every man signs."

The Saints signed willingly, but the Strangers held back until Miles Standish stomped forward, sword clanking at his side, and grabbed the quill pen. "Law and order are necessary," he said gruffly, "if you're going to run a colony!" After he signed, the rest of the able-bodied Strangers stepped forward one by one. Even John Billington signed. Merrie would have signed, too, but women were forbidden to write their names on the document. Merrie didn't think it was fair that the women shouldn't have an equal say in the laws. After all, they were expected to do an equal amount of work! But she kept prudently quiet as another vote was taken, unanimously electing John Carver governor of the new colony.

Captain Jones ordered the anchor dropped. Sailors leaped eagerly to their work and spun the capstan, lustily singing a sea chantey.

"Heigh ho-o-o-o-o, up she rises
Heigh ho-o-o-o-o, up she rises, early in the
    morning.
Whachu gonna do-o-o with a drunken sailor
Put him in the longboat and make him bail
    'er
Earlee in the morning
Heigh ho, up she rises
Heigh ho-o-o, up she rises
Earlee in the morning."

Back in the first harbor, Merrie couldn't wait to set her feet on the sandy beach that gleamed pristine white in the morning sun. A sea gull screamed overhead, and Merrie wanted to embrace the whole wide world. Land! Land, at last!

Chapter Seven

IN the next month Merrie went ashore only once, and that was to wash clothes with the other women. She looked at her rough red hands and thought, I scrub clothes, while the men get to search for a suitable place to live and the boys gather firewood and dig clams.

She had lived on the boat a month now, and during that time Susanna White had given birth to a baby boy, naming him Peregrine. A very appropriate name, she thought, for it meant "pilgrim." However, the joyful birth was overshadowed by Dorothy Bradford's death when she was found drowned alongside the *Mayflower*. Some believed she had thrown herself over the side in despair, but others maintained she'd slipped and fallen into the bay. Merrie wept for the sad-eyed woman, but she knew that now at least Dorothy Bradford's sorrow was over.

Today the exploring expedition had come in early, and Zack joined her at the ship's rail. He was chuckling to himself, and she glared at him. While he explored the forests and rivers, she had been stuck on the *Mayflower*!

Zack's grin was contagious, and Merrie smiled in spite of herself. But her smile faded when she noticed the lines around his mouth and circles under his eyes. His lean face was thinner and his cheekbones more prominent.

"You look pale, Zack," she commented.

"Are you concerned?" he asked. He coughed slightly.

"It was just a comment," she said, trying to conceal her worry.

His face took on a dark, brooding look. "There isn't anyone who doesn't have a cold or bad cough. Seems as if I'll never get warm! Or dry!" He laughed ruefully. "The campfires don't keep us warm at night and wading ashore every day in that icy water keeps us wet all day."

She yearned to reach out to Zack.

"I guess it isn't much fun for you either, Zack," she said, realizing everyone suffered in this miserable weather. She kicked at the bucket. "It's almost Christmas, and we're not on land yet and haven't even started to build cabins!" She knew she shouldn't complain, but she couldn't help herself. How could she face one more day on this wretched ship?

"I have a feeling we'll find the colony site tomorrow!" Zack said confidently.

She hoped he was right, but when she

glanced at him, she couldn't keep the doubt from her eyes.

Nonetheless, she should have believed Zack, for the very next day, December 21st, a place was chosen, and the *Mayflower* sailed across the calm waters from Provincetown to Plymouth. Plymouth! what a perfect name, she thought. A name chosen by John Smith in 1614 and the same name as the place they'd started from in England. Yesterday's despair turned to buoyant happiness as Merrie gazed at the shoreline that was to be her new home!

The shallop, or big boat, took one load of passengers after another to shore. When Merrie's turn came, Zack helped her into the boat. She couldn't keep her teeth from chattering, and when she grasped the bowlines, they were coated with ice. But she didn't care! She'd rather walk through freezing water and be drenched by cold rain than stay on the ship another minute!

She waved happily at Luke, who stayed on ship to mend sails but promised to come ashore soon.

Coming close to the beach, they dropped anchor in the shallow water. Zack helped her into the icy water to wade ashore, but she didn't feel the cold. Her eyes were fastened on the land before her. The land that was to be her home! "Oh, Zack," she said breathlessly, "isn't it wonderful to be alive? Let's run in the woods. It's been so long since I stretched my legs."

He smiled, and his dark face shone. "You're

not washing clothes?" he asked as he took long strides beside her.

"Mistress Sedgewick said I could help later," she said, almost glad she had someone to answer to. So much for her sought-after independence!

When they reached the beach, Merrie ran ahead of Zack and reached down to grab a fistful of sand, letting the tiny grains slowly trickle through her slender fingers. "One run," she pleaded, glancing back at Zack, "to get my land legs back. That's all I ask. When I come back here, I'll pound clothes till my hands turn blue." Her eyes sparkled. "One run, Zack?" she coaxed.

"I wish I could," he said, eyeing her shining face, "but I don't think I could keep up with your bubbling spirits. The way I feel now, you'd outdistance me in five minutes. Besides," he added, grinning at her, "I'm supposed to join Brewster and the others to plot out where the Common House will be built."

"Isn't it exciting?" she asked, twirling about. "I have a place to stay, and, oh, Zack, this is my new home!" She held her arms wide as if to embrace the entire forest and distant hills.

"Hmmm, I like the way you hide your joy, Merrie," he teased, and tilted up her chin with his forefinger. "You live up to your name, you know."

She smiled, deeply breathing in the crisp air. "Who wouldn't be happy that we've finally decided to build here."

"Oliver Loomis?" Zack suggested dryly.

"Ugh!" Merrie screwed up her face. "Every time that man comes by, he snarls at me. Why does he dislike me so much?"

"You were a stowaway," Zack said simply, "and you've been accepted by most of the Pilgrims and don't let things get you down." He grinned wickedly. "Not even Loomis's sour face." He touched her nose. "Don't worry about Master Loomis. Go and have your run, Merrie. We'll talk later." With a cheery wave he hurried away.

Although she'd miss Zack, she still glowed with a warm happiness as she turned to the woods. Fastening her cloak, she felt a deep sense of peace and contentment well up inside. How wonderful it was to be alone after months of living on a cramped ship.

She gave a skip, then picked up her skirts and raced wildly to a distant big oak. Along the beaten path she ran pell-mell, wondering who had made this trail. She knew the men had spotted Indians, but were they friends or enemies? And were they watching her now? Warily, she glanced about, but all she saw was a black squirrel skittering up a tree. Even though the winter sky was bleak, the day was glorious. She stayed in the woods longer than she'd intended. Mistress Sedgewick wouldn't be happy.

"Merrie!"

She would know Luke's deep voice anywhere. She stopped, waiting.

The short husky sailor soon caught up with

her, crashing through the underbrush. He wore a wool doublet and a striped scarf tied around his neck, and at his side he carried a flintlock, its muzzle pointed at the ground. "I thought you'd be with Zack Gaines," he said, giving her a dazzling smile, "and I'm glad you're not." He paused. "You see, I wanted to be alone with you first."

She smiled, too, pleased at his remark. She touched the musket. "Do you shoot, Luke?"

"Not very well," he admitted. "I'm a sailor, not a hunter. But I can give you a few pointers with Robert Coppin's gun."

"The second mate has a gun?" she asked, surprised.

He nodded, winking. "He's got to keep us sea devils in line one way or another, doesn't he?" Chuckling, he handed her the gun. "Try and shoot it." He folded his arms across his barrel chest and waited.

Gingerly, she took the musket, feeling its sleek lines. "I-I can't."

"Here," he said gruffly. "I'm no expert, but I know how to hold it. Press the stock snug against your cheek and aim at that poplar over there."

Several times she fired, and not once did she hit the target. Each time it felt as if a mule had kicked her in the shoulder.

"It's harder than it looks," she said. "And I guess it's time to go back." They turned and walked in silence back up the path. Merrie still held the musket, carefully.

"Shoot, Merrie!" Luke suddenly yelled,

pointing at a wild turkey that half flew and half ran along the dead leaves.

Before she could think, she hoisted the heavy gun to her shoulder, aimed, and fired. The gun's kick propelled her back against a tree, but not before she saw the heavy bird flop to the ground and remain still.

Luke threw back his red head and chortled. "One shot and pow, you kill a turkey! Good girl!" He gave her an admiring look and grinned, his freckles dominating his rosy cheeks. "Remember that Greek myth you told me last week? About Diana, the huntress? Well, I should call you 'Merry Diana'!" He picked up the dead turkey and handed it to her. "Here's your kill," he said proudly. "The Sedgewicks should appreciate fresh meat!"

She gave Luke a broad smile. "I don't know how I did it," she marveled, looking at the turkey in astonishment and shaking her head. "Now, I'd really better get back, Luke. There's a mound of washing waiting for me."

"Then, let's go," Luke said jauntily, but he didn't move, standing directly in her path.

Surprised, Merrie studied Luke's round smiling face, pinched red by the cold.

Gently, he pushed back her hood, letting her golden hair flow loosely over her shoulders. "You're a beautiful girl, Merrie Courtland," he said softly. "Strong, too." His fingers gently trailed down her cheek, and for a moment she closed her eyes. All feeling was blotted out except for a warm sensation when she gazed into Luke's clear blue eyes.

He took her hand and lightly said, "Come back to England with me, Merrie. Don't stay in this cold forsaken place!"

"Luke," she said, flustered. "I can't go back." Then laughing shakily, she added, "After all, I just arrived, and I can't very well turn around and go right back." She stepped away, walking forward along the path.

Luke gave a low chuckle. "I'll wager you'll change your mind before I sail," he said, swaggering alongside her.

She laughed again. "Such self-confidence, Luke!" But she was glad he wasn't angry at her refusal.

Arriving at the makeshift camp where women, by the shore, pounded clothes clean, she parted from Luke. Walking with a spring to her step she hurried over to Patience Sedgewick, unable to hide her happy grin. "I brought fresh meat for our supper," she said gleefully, offering the turkey to Mistress Patience.

Patience Sedgewick, bent over her washing, gave Merrie a startled look, glancing from the young girl to the turkey. She bit her underlip, saying nothing.

Bewildered, Merrie stood watching Patience squeeze water from a blouse.

Oliver Loomis, standing nearby, rushed forward, his long grasshopper legs pumping furiously. "You mean you shot that turkey?" he shouted, the veins in his neck standing out like blue cords. Angrily, he snatched the turkey from her hand and flung it to the ground. "A girl shooting a gun! Who ever heard of such a thing!" He loomed tall and menacing above her. "I knew you were no good from the first day you skulked aboard the ship! Hiding like a common criminal!" He glared at her, his pale eyes glittering. "You probably are a criminal," he added.

"You shouldn't have gone into the woods, Merrie," Patience said in a quavery voice. "And shooting a musket. Daniel will be displeased."

"But I didn't do anything wrong," Merrie protested weakly, throwing out her hands in a helpless gesture. Suddenly she felt a pang of fear. Was Patience sorry she'd offered to give her a home?

"Of course she shouldn't have gone hunting," Oliver Loomis repeated icily. "Any decent girl would have known better. I can tell you right now, Mistress Sedgewick, that you've made a serious mistake in inviting this viper into your house!" His black coat and high collar only accentuated his cadaverous face. "Mark my words, she'll heap shame and ridicule on you!" He sneeringly looked Merrie up and down. "Look at her! Unbound hair, flushed face, blood on her hands! She's a barbarian!"

Merrie felt color rush to her cheeks and had to bite off a sharp retort. Her chest was so heavy that she felt as if she were suffocating. Perhaps Master Loomis was right. No matter what she did, it was wrong!

Chapter Eight

ALL of Merrie's hard work on the *Mayflower* and the saving of Patience Sedgewick's life were wiped away simply because she'd shot a musket. Oliver Loomis wasn't the only one who had been shocked at her behavior. After a month she still felt alone and isolated. Often when she casually glanced up, she found people watching her with narrow eyes. Then they'd hastily look away. She was rarely spoken to and went about her work silently. Daniel Sedgewick had ordered her not to touch a musket ever again and reminded her that if she was to live with them, she must be obedient and learn a woman's work.

Poor Master Sedgewick. He was now lying in the Common House, stricken by the "general sickness." Merrie was glad she had apologized to him, even if she felt what she'd done wasn't a crime. He'd accepted her apology indifferently, although Zack and some of the

Elders had forgiven her, along with Captain Jones and the sailors.

The crewmen were even friendlier, and it was obvious the rift between sailors and Saints had gradually healed. The crewmen came to admire the Pilgrims' courage and were grateful for their help when sickness also spread through their ranks.

One January afternoon as Merrie searched for berries she tried to forget how she was shunned. It felt good to be in the forest where a light snow dusted the ground and fir tree boughs. She wished she could return with a whole basket of blueberries so Master Sedgewick would have a treat, but only a few tenacious berries clung to the barren branches.

Merrie, numb with cold, decided to turn back with her few pitiful berries. Besides, it was time to relieve Patience, who almost had to be dragged from her husband's bedside.

Entering the settlement, Merrie caught sight of the thatched roof on the Common House. The large community center reassured her, for it gave the bleak shoreline a semblance of civilization. Down First Street she walked, past Bradford's completed frame house and by the staked-out plots of soon-to-be-built houses.

Zack ran toward her, looking lean and grim in his dark doublet, boots, and hat. "Merrie," he said, reaching her side and grasping her hand, "you must be brave."

Her heart leaped. What now? she thought.

Could things get any worse? "What's wrong?" she asked, barely able to get the words past her closed throat. Fearfully she examined his handsome face.

"Daniel Sedgewick died an hour ago," he said softly. "Patience is with Mary Brewster in the Common House."

She uttered a low moan. "Oh, Zack, not Master Sedgewick! What will Patience do?"

"Patience will survive, especially with you at her side," he replied, wearily pushing back his wide-brimmed hat. "Master Sedgewick is the twentieth one to be buried in thirty days."

Her eyes stung with tears when she thought of Master Sedgewick's burial tonight. A grave would be dug at midnight, and no marker would show where his resting place was. There were no gravestones on Cole's Hill. That way no Indians would know how many Pilgrims had died.

A few prayers would be mumbled over his body, and then he'd quickly be lowered into a black hole. Merrie's nerves throbbed at the image, and she was so tired. Touching her forehead, she swayed slightly.

Immediately, Zack reached for her. "Merrie, don't get sick, please," he pleaded.

Wanly, she smiled at him, pleased at his concern. "I'll try not to, but I don't know why I should be the only one spared this winter. I wish for once I could feel warm and cozy and eat my fill of a hot meal."

She held out the berries. "Take these," she

whispered. "Master Sedgewick won't need them now." Her voice caught in her throat. "I'm too late."

"Merrie, it looks as if you could use a mug of hot soup." With his arm still around her they walked slowly to the Common House.

She looked gratefully at Zack. "Why don't you shun me like everyone else?"

"I admire you," he said matter-of-factly. "You've hardly slept in your rush to nurse the sick. You know," he said gently, "it takes time to change people's opinions. You can't do it all at once." His ebony eyes shone with tenderness, then he grinned and said, "Look at me. I didn't think I could ever learn to like a 'stowaway girl.'"

Somehow this time she didn't mind his nickname for her. Zack continued, brushing back a flyaway curl on her cheek, "And I'm not the only one you've impressed. You've got a toughness beneath that fragile appearance that I'll bet you didn't even know you had." He glanced down at her, a small smile playing about his lips. "I just wish you weren't so skinny and pale."

"I'll mix a little ground sage, fat, and cornmeal," she said, her mouth puckering at the thought of the vile taste, "and be as good as new."

He chuckled. "I know you will," he said lightly. But underneath his banter was a somber note as he left her at the Common House entrance.

Entering the large room with its rows of

sickbeds, Merrie glimpsed Master Bradford hurrying toward her.

"I'm sorry, Merrie," he said, "but Master Sedgewick went so fast that we couldn't get word to you before. Patience is mourning in the corner and needs you."

Merrie wanted to cry, but no tears would come. She and Daniel Sedgewick hadn't been that close to each other.

"Go to Mistress Patience, Merrie," he said compassionately. "See what you can do for her."

Merrie nodded, turning away to join Mistress Patience. Gently she placed her hand over hers. "Be brave, Mistress Patience," she said softly, aching to put her arms around her, but something held Patience aloof from any emotion. Even her eyes were dry.

"Daniel was a good man," she said, removing her hand from Merrie's and folding her hands in her lap. "We were going to have a wonderful life in the New World. Now the dream is ended." Her voice was empty, and she stared at Merrie with unseeing eyes.

In the next few weeks Patience stoically went about her cooking and weaving while Merrie worked in the hospital, helping Zack and Doctor Fuller. She mixed herbs, carried water until she thought she couldn't move another step, and washed bedding. She even helped gather firewood, since most of the able-bodied men were sick.

At night she was so exhausted she just fell into bed without eating. And even then she slept fitfully. Her thoughts tumbled and twisted with images of the dead and dying. Ten more men and four women had died, including Rose, Miles Standish's wife. Of the eighteen women, only five were left. Often Merrie wakened with cold chills and tears streaming down her cheeks.

In February a boatload of sailors were brought in from the *Mayflower*. Half the crew had died, and the survivors called the *Mayflower* the "plague ship." Watching the litters, Merrie's heart caught in her throat as she glimpsed flaming red hair, which she'd recognize any place! Luke! Not the brawny swaggering sailor who was so invincible!

Merrie snatched a jar of herbs from the shelf and hurried to his side.

"Hello, Merrie," he said weakly, licking his parched lips.

"Luke Bosworth," she scolded, "what are you doing here!" She sprinkled the rose leaves and fruit of the rose into her palm. "Here," she said, "take this."

Luke grimaced and said, "Get me some ale to wash it down."

She ran for the precious ale reserved only for the sick and came back with a full mug, lifting Luke's head so he could drink.

Finishing the ale, he lay back down, perspiration dotting his forehead. "I've missed you, Merrie," he said, and propped himself up on his elbows. "But we've been busy getting the ship ready to sail back to England."

Her heart lurched. She didn't want Luke to leave. He was her friend and, she thought unhappily, she needed all the friends she could get. "How can you leave in winter?" she asked, a catch in her voice.

Luke, showing even white teeth, winked and said with his old bravado, "You wouldn't miss me, would you, Merrie?"

"Yes, I would," she admitted, tucking a blanket about his legs.

"We sail next month," he said. "And, take my word for it, you're not going to miss me."

"I won't?" she asked, hands on her hips. "And how do you know what I will or won't do?"

"Because you'll be on the *Mayflower* with me!" he answered promptly.

When Luke closed his eyes, she hurried to find Doctor Fuller in the East Room, where he leaned over Susanna White with his hand on her forehead. Susanna couldn't get sick, Merrie thought. She just couldn't. Not when her husband, William, had recently died. Not when she had to take care of Peregrine, her newborn baby, and also her five-year-old son, Resolved.

"Doctor Fuller," Merrie interrupted, touching his sleeve. "Will you please come and look at Luke Bosworth? He's one of the sailors who were just brought in."

"After I treat Mistress White," he said curtly, examining Susanna's tongue.

"He — he looks very ill," she persisted worriedly.

"Zack," Doctor Fuller said in exasperation, "go over and check on him, will you?"

"Come on, Merrie," Zack said, taking her elbow. "Let's see how sick your sailor really is." He gave her a speculative sidelong look. "This Luke must be special to you."

"He — he is," she said, hating herself for stammering again, but she didn't know how Zack would react to Luke. "He's one of the few friends I have," she ended lamely.

"I see," said Zack slowly.

No, you don't see at all, she thought, but she felt further explanations would be useless.

From the time Luke got sick until he recovered a week later, Zack didn't go near him, except for that first day when she had been so frightened. Taking a moment from her nursing, Merrie gazed over the frozen Jones River, named for Captain Jones. She was puzzled. Surely Zack couldn't be jealous of Luke?

Now that Luke was again working on the *Mayflower*, readying the ship for the return voyage, she wondered if perhaps he wasn't right. Perhaps she should go back to England as he'd so flippantly told her she would. She missed Nancy, her best friend. In this wilderness she hadn't one girl friend to share secrets with or to laugh with. She sighed. It had been so long since she'd laughed.

Merrie glanced down at her tattered dress. If she were home, this would have been discarded long ago. But now she must patch it again or clout it, as the Pilgrims said. She remembered the words of an old Pilgrim ballad:

And now our garments begin to grow thin,
And wool is much wanted to card and to spin;
If we can get a garment to cover without,
Our other in-garments are clout upon clout;
Our clothes we brought with us are often
    torn,
They need to be clouted before they are
    worn. . . .

"Doctor Fuller said you'd gone for a walk by the river," came a deep, rich voice.

Startled, she wheeled about and was delighted to see Zack grinning at her. He was dressed in black, from his boots to his hat, but over his shoulder were flung two pairs of shiny skates.

"Zack," she said, astonished he'd bothered to find her. "Are those your ice skates?"

"This pair is," he said, sitting down on a nearby stump and strapping on the wooden runners over his soles. He looked up. "This pair, though, is yours." He offered her the new pair.

Her eyes widened.

Zack threw back his head and laughed. "Merrie, when you get excited, your brown eyes light up like amber flames."

"For me?" she asked delightedly as she ran her fingers over the smooth blades.

"For you," Zack replied, "made by the ship's carpenter."

"What makes you think I can ice-skate?" She glanced at him impishly, feeling girlishly happy again. How little it took to make her joyful these days, she thought.

"A girl like you? Why, you're as graceful as a deer and born to ice-skate." He nodded. "Go on," he urged. "Put them on."

For a moment she could only stare at them, remembering the time she'd skated on the Thames River, whirling and twirling about. "Oh, Zack, thank you," she said excitedly. Without a moment's delay she sank down on the riverbank and tried them on. "They fit perfectly."

"Good!" he said. "It's about time we put some roses back in your cheeks." His dark eyes appraised her approvingly.

"And do you ice-skate, Zack?" she questioned, thinking it strange a Pilgrim would engage in such a frivolous activity.

He stood up and skated onto the silver river. He moved effortlessly backward. "I skate," he said simply, cutting a wide figure eight. "It's one of the vices I picked up living in Holland."

It had been a long time since she'd been on skates, and she wobbily skated out onto the slick ice. Zack was at her side in an instant, helping her.

Soon they were skating arm in arm up the long river and around a bend. How glorious it felt to be skimming over the smooth, glistening surface in Zack's arms.

Together, their arms crisscrossed in front

of them and holding hands, they glided down-river. When they rounded a bend in the river, Merrie gasped. An Indian was standing motionless on a hill, silently watching them.

"Guess we came farther than I thought," Zack said casually, wheeling easily around in a wide arc. Merrie's heart hammered at the sight of her first Indian, but she had to admit as she glanced back, that he didn't look too forbidding. Only tall and stately.

Returning to the riverbank from where they'd started, Zack unstrapped her skates, then pulled her to her feet. They walked slowly through the quiet forest, the pine trees heavy with snow, and back toward Plymouth. The sunny day, the exhilarating frost in the air, and skating with Zack had made her forget her dismal backbreaking weeks of nursing sick and dying people.

"What are you thinking, Merrie?" Zack said, an amused expression on his face when he looked down at her.

An answering smile flickered across her lips when she looked into the depths of his black eyes, arched by thick dark brows. "I'm thinking," she responded happily, "what a perfect day this has been."

Zack stopped, facing her. "The day was perfect, wasn't it? And do you know why?" Before she could answer, he said, "You, Merrie Courtland," lightly touching her cheek with his gloved hand.

Merrie thought surely his burning imprint would be left on her face.

Zack gave a low chuckle. "I've never known anyone like you, 'stowaway girl.'"

She stared at him with sparkling eyes while her slow heartbeat thundered in her ears.

"Will you go ice skating with me again?" he asked.

She nodded and hoped her head didn't bob too eagerly.

Swiftly, Zack lowered his dark head, and Merrie thought surely his lips would touch hers, but instead he pulled back, his eyes softening. "How about tomorrow, 'stowaway girl'? Same place?"

"Yes," she whispered, unable to take her eyes from his lean good looks. How she wished he would kiss her. However, she said evenly, "Tomorrow will be fine."

"Tomorrow," he repeated, and they walked the rest of the way in silence, each one lost in thought.

But the next day Merrie was not well enough to go ice skating or even get out of bed. She ached in every joint, her head throbbing agonizingly. Her body was on fire, and her clothes were soaked through with sweat. She sank back on her bed. "Oh, God, help me," she prayed, closing her eyes and moaning softly, "I've got the 'general sickness.'"

Chapter Nine

DOCTOR Fuller placed his hand on Merrie's burning forehead and shook his head. "You're to stay in bed," he ordered.

"But I-I can't," she protested weakly, trying to sit up. "I promised I'd read to...." Her voice trailed off, and Doctor Fuller's image faded. Dizzily she sank back on her pillow, feeling waves of nausea wash over her.

"Rest!" Doctor Fuller said severely, pulling the blanket up to her chin.

She shut her eyes, trying to fight down the sour bile that rose in her mouth.

"Under no circumstances are you to get up!" Doctor Fuller commanded. "Understood?"

Unable to answer, she feebly raised her hand in agreement. She couldn't get up if she tried, she thought. She simply had to lie here and let the room swirl around her.

"I'll come by later," the doctor said, but

his faint words sounded as if they came from a long tunnel. She shut her eyes, feeling herself spinning and floating down it.

Later, when her eyes again fluttered open, Mistress Patience was seated by her side. The middle-aged woman clutched her blue cape at the throat, and her gray eyes intently observed Merrie. "Merrie," she asked anxiously, "how do you feel?"

"Awful," she replied shakily, struggling against the queasiness that rose and fell in her stomach. "How — how long have I been asleep?"

"Two days."

"Two days?" Merrie whispered in disbelief.

Patience reached for a bowl. "You must eat," she said, dipping a spoon into the bowl.

"What is it?" Merrie asked, eyeing the spoon suspiciously.

"Rabbit stew."

Merrie shook her head. "No," she intoned. "I can't."

"Merrie, please try," Mistress Patience pleaded. "You've been without food for two days." Wearily, she pushed back a strand of gray hair that straggled loose from her white cap. "One spoonful," she coaxed and pressed her thin lips together, moving the spoon toward Merrie's mouth. Merrie had seen that determined look before and knew she must make an effort.

Mistress Patience touched Merrie's shoulder. "I don't want to lose you, too," she said shakily, and tears brimmed in her gray sad eyes.

"All right," Merrie said in a low voice, swallowing a spoonful to please her. She forced down another mouthful. "No more," she begged, waving back the food. She lay down, shivering and chilled to the bone.

"There, there, Merrie." Mistress Patience stood. "Go back to sleep." With a gentle pat on Merrie's cheek, she turned and left.

Merrie stared at the ceiling but soon drifted off into a restless sleep. Her head danced with strange images and dreams.

Once she jerked awake only to find the Common House as dark and damp as a cave and no one in sight. She relived a terrible dream in which Oliver Loomis had chased her into the woods. He waved a musket overhead, and when they reached the frozen river, she raced onto the thin ice. Under her weight, the ice cracked, then shattered, and opened beneath her, plummeting her down, down into the river's icy depths. When she frantically clawed her way toward the surface, she couldn't find the open water. Struggling, she tried to break the ice-roof, but it held firm. Suddenly ice water poured into her nostrils, her throat, and mouth. In her ears roared Oliver Loomis's laughter.

But it was a dream. Turning her head, she gazed out the window, focusing on the black leaden sky, a sky as blank and dull as her spirits.

She shuddered as a spasm rippled through her thin frame. "Z-Zack," she called, but the word was more like a hoarse croak. She wondered if she were about to die. Pain gripped her, and she whimpered, wishing she could die. She clenched the sheets between her fingers, teeth chattering. The New World, she thought bitterly, had brought nothing but pain and grief! Then into the dim recesses of her brain crept the bright image of ice skating with Zack. Momentarily comforted, she once again sank into a deep sleep.

When she awakened, Luke sat beside her, stroking her hand. For a moment she was confused, expecting Zack.

"Luke," she whispered.

"I'm right here." He bent over, wiping her wet forehead with a cloth.

Even though the nausea had vanished, she felt as weak as a day-old kitten. She looked at Luke. "I'm hungry," she said, licking her cracked lips.

"Yup," he said with a lopsided grin. "You're getting better."

Mistress Patience, hovering in the background, immediately hurried forward with bread and a dried apple. "Here, dear, eat this." Merrie thought the lines in Patience Sedgewick's face had softened. How pretty she once must have been, Merrie thought.

Merrie chewed the apple, relishing the taste, but even more than the apple, she relished the sound of Mistress Patience calling her "dear."

Luke reached over and tousled her hair. "I was plenty scared, Merrie."

"You were?" she asked, eyes wide with surprise. Someone did care if she lived or died.

"You bet I was," he said, grabbing her hand and squeezing.

Her heart jumped when Zack approached. "Merrie," he said happily, "I'm glad to see you awake." The charming smile that she loved radiated from his dark face. However, when he noticed Luke's hand on hers, his smile vanished.

Quietly Merrie withdrew her hand, thrusting it under the covers. "I-I was hoping you'd come, Zack," she said tremulously.

"Of course I'd come," he said, his smile reappearing. "Did you ever doubt me?"

"No, I didn't doubt you." How could she ever doubt him when he looked at her that way?

Zack placed his cool fingers to her brow. "No fever," he said approvingly. "I prescribe lots of rest. In a few weeks I predict you'll be planting a vegetable garden."

She smiled back at him, almost forgetting Luke was standing at her side.

"No, no," Luke interjected, grinning insolently at Zack. "She'll soon be well enough to sail on the *Mayflower*."

Zack's expression didn't change, but tiny golden flames leaped to his eyes. "That's for Merrie to decide, isn't it?" he asked levelly.

"Sure is," Luke agreed jauntily, laying a

possessive hand on Merrie's shoulder.

"Well, I see you're in good hands," Zack said. "I'll leave you two alone." Then, with fingers touching his black curls, he gave her a mock salute and moved on.

With hurt eyes and a twist in her heart, she watched him depart.

It was another week before Merrie had recovered enough to help with the washing and cooking, but even so, Mistress Patience insisted she rest at least two hours every day.

Today, sitting on a bench before the Common House, Merrie soaked up the March sun. All around her people were busy. Men thatched the roof of the small cottage where she and Patience would soon move. Others made furniture, including John Alden, an excellent carpenter, who was putting finishing touches on a three-legged stool. To the west, a dozen men cleared land for plowing. She recognized John Carver in his brilliant crimson cloak, sawing down a sapling. A few men plowed clearings, which meant gardens could be planted next month. While Patience baked bread in the outdoor clay oven, and Susanna White washed clothes, she sat lazily watching them. She looked again at the small hut that would be her home. The roof of dried cattails was almost completed. How good it would feel to be out of the bustling Common House and have a little privacy.

With a pang, she thought of Zack. She knew Doctor Fuller didn't need his help any longer now that the plague seemed to be over, but where had he been all week? Perhaps he was setting traps, getting ready to begin his fur trade. But it was strange he hadn't visited her at least once. She missed him. On the other hand, Luke was constantly with her, always attentive and always urging her to come back with him on the *Mayflower*.

She leaned back, closing her eyes, glad the bitterly cold winter was over. Oh, she realized, there'd be wintry days ahead, but they wouldn't last long.

"I see you're idle once again, Merrie Courtland," Oliver Loomis snarled, observing her through slitted eyes. "If I were you, I'd get to work. Your presence is rather temporary here!" His half smile didn't touch his cold eyes.

"I have been helping," she said indignantly. "I've worked with the sick, I've cooked and . . ." but she abruptly stopped. What was the use explaining anything to this hateful man?

Oliver Loomis crossed his arms, and a sly smile played about his too-thin lips. "Oh, yes, you've wormed your way into Patience Sedgewick's house, and now you're trying to fool others into letting you remain. But I'm not fooled by your clever ways," he said, jabbing his thumb against his black frock coat, "and neither are most of the Pilgrims."

Her spirits fell. Oliver Loomis was right. She didn't have many friends. Most colonists still shied away from her.

"Being on the Council of Elders, I intend to

see you're shipped back on the *Mayflower*!"
His raspy laugh sent a chill up her spine.
"Preferably the way you came!" He shook a
long finger at her.

She scrambled to her feet, lifting her chin
proudly. When she'd first met Master Loomis,
she'd cowered before him, but she'd been
through too much not to stand up for herself.
"I have no intention of going back to England," she said, refusing to be intimidated.

"What are you afraid of?" he asked softly,
watching her carefully. "Why did you run
away?"

She tried to keep her rising panic from
showing. Had she committed a crime in
running away from a hateful marriage? If
this man ever found out, what would he do to
her? Put her in stocks until the *Mayflower*
sailed?

"Why would you stay in Plymouth where
you're not wanted?" the skinny man questioned, stroking his beard thoughtfully.

She found it difficult not to retreat from
the naked hate that glittered from Master
Loomis's yellowish-gray eyes.

"Don't think you can escape from the
Council!" he threatened.

All at once a drumroll sounded. With big
eyes she glanced at Oliver Loomis. What was
it? Only on Sundays did the drumbeat call
Pilgrims to church at the Common House.

Then she saw the reason. A tall Indian
walked sedately down the main road, coming
directly toward her.

Chapter Ten

WILLIAM Bradford came out of the Common House and stood in the doorway, warily watching the Indian. The scantily clad warrior, wearing only a leather loincloth, had brilliant slashes of yellow paint on each cheek and a feathered headband. An Indian, Merrie thought. What would happen now? Some of the colonists moved backward, including Oliver Loomis, who, with his mouth open, rapidly backed against a tree.

Miles Standish, brandishing his gun, came running. "Back! Stay back, everyone," he shouted at the onlookers.

The Indian merely smiled, gazing about mildly. His brown eyes and lean face were calm. "Welcome," he said, turning back to Master Bradford, who was joined by Governor Carver. "I come as your friend, and my name is Samoset."

Merrie stared at this English-speaking

Indian. How strange to hear him speak in their own language!

"And you are welcome to Plymouth," John Carver replied.

"Merrie," he went on, "will you bring us ale?" He eyed the bare-chested Indian. "And a coat for Samoset. He must be freezing."

Merrie rushed inside to pour out some ale and to snatch a coat off the door hook. This was the first Indian she'd seen up close, and she didn't want to miss a minute. She dashed back outside.

After drinking the ale, the three men went into the Common House where other Elders waited to confer with the Indian. When they finally emerged from their long conference, the sun had set.

Stephen Hopkins, his arm around Samoset, announced proudly, "Samoset will be staying with me tonight."

Suspicious, Miles Standish marched forward. "I'll stand guard outside your door."

Samoset shrugged his broad shoulders. "You do not need to." He held out his empty hands. "I have no weapon. But," he added, "that is up to you."

Miles Standish, dressed in armor, clanked glumly after them.

Merrie still found it hard to believe that after the countless times the Elders had tried to contact the Indians, one of them had strolled into Plymouth as unafraid and nonchalant as if he belonged here.

The next morning, Merrie watched Samoset

come out of Stephen Hopkins's house, holding up his gifts. Each one, a knife, a bracelet, and a silver ring, glinted in the sun. In return, Samoset promised to bring back more Indians to help the colonists.

The next day, true to his word, Samoset brought back five warriors. Merrie glimpsed Zack, using sign language, parleying with an Indian who held five beaver skins. Oh, Zack would make a fine fur trader all right, she thought. Already he was laughing with the Indians, and it was obvious they liked him. Yes, he'd be very successful. It certainly was clear that he was more interested in trading with Indians than he was in bothering with a "stowaway girl"!

But Merrie tried not to think about Zack and kept herself busy. Today she and Mistress Patience were sewing a new dress that had been cut from a bolt of navy gingham dotted with tiny red flowers, which Mary Brewster had given her. Merrie smiled. Mary Brewster was probably as sick of seeing her in her ragged, torn clouted dress as she was of wearing it.

Merrie held the half-finished dress up to herself, pleased at the reflection in the cracked mirror. Color was gradually coming back in her cheeks, and the dark material enhanced her long blond hair, making it appear like molten gold in the shaft of light coming through the cabin's open window.

"Oh, isn't it beautiful?" Merrie asked, climbing up on a chair, slipping into the skirt, and standing on a chair so Mistress Patience could measure the hem.

"Don't be vain," Mistress Patience said quietly, pinning the cloth. "Turn."

Merrie laughed. She felt comfortable with somber Patience Sedgewick now. Together they cooked, mended, and had made the cabin cozy with new curtains and a woven reed rug for the dirt floor. Mistress Patience was still sober and spent much of her time in prayer, but Merrie had grown to like her and knew that Patience liked her, too. She felt sorry for Patience, though, knowing she still grieved for Daniel.

Merrie got down from the chair and went back to her fireplace bench to continue stitching her sleeve. She glanced at Patience, whose white-capped head was lowered silently over the hem she basted. How lonely her life must be, Merrie thought. The life of a widow. "Widow Sedgewick," as she was now called. Merrie grimly tightened her lips. To think that when she'd first arrived in the New World she had vowed to be independent and not ask for help. Especially from people who disliked her. But now she could understand how impossible it was to isolate herself. In Plymouth you had to depend on your neighbors just to survive.

Merrie took a shaky breath at the memory of all the sickness and death she had witnessed. No, she thought, she no longer wanted to be alone. She yearned to be with someone, someone with whom she could share things and laugh. She wondered if Patience wanted this, too. Letting her sewing fall in her lap, her thoughts once again strayed to Zack. She missed him.

Luke kept her busy and helped her forget Zack. His visits were a daily occurrence now that he'd soon be sailing, and this morning was no exception. "Hello, Merrie," he said, sauntering to her side. "Let's go over to the Common House. Chief Massasoit will be arriving soon, and the Indians are already dancing in celebration."

Hastily, Merrie put aside her sewing. She loved watching the Indians' reactions to how the colonists lived. They were curious about everything and very friendly.

In the Common House, five Indians, wearing long leather leggings, their faces painted in bright reds, greens, and blues with black stripes decorating their cheeks, danced to the loud beat of a tom-tom. One brave had a foxtail trailing down the back of his head, but others wore feathers.

Pleased, Samoset stood nearby with his friend Squanto, watching the festivities. Squanto had chosen to live at Plymouth. He'd been sold into slavery in Spain, escaped to London, and come back to New England with Captain John Smith. From across the room Squanto caught Merrie's eye, and he grinned and waved exuberantly. He often talked to Merrie.

She waved back, feeling a warm friendship

with this brave, who was as tall and straight as a poplar. But when he started to come toward her, a cannon boomed and he stopped. His startled expression was replaced by a gleeful whoop as he spun about and raced outdoors. Merrie and Luke hurriedly followed.

When she was outside in the bright sun, she shielded her eyes and stared at the hill where the ship's cannons were mounted. Why, she wondered, had the biggest cannon been fired?

She soon found out. Edward Winslow, the youngest Elder, came running down the street. "Chief Massasoit has arrived!"

Merrie craned her neck for a look, squinting down the road. Suddenly, she saw the great sachem and his warriors, and she caught her breath. Slowly and to the beat of a drum, they walked into Plymouth.

The bronzed chief, regal-looking, had well-oiled skin that gleamed in the bright sun. Massasoit was Indian royalty and not at all like English royalty.

Chief Massasoit held up his palm in a friendly salute when Governor Carver approached. The Indian's long face, dyed a deep mulberry, contrasted sharply with the white bone chain about his neck.

A green feather poked above his black coarse hair, which was parted down the middle and braided in two long plaits that draped over his massive chest. Behind the chief were at least fifty or sixty fierce-looking warriors. Merrie's heart lurched painfully. So many Indians, she thought, and hoped they didn't realize they outnumbered the settlers four to one. She noticed she wasn't the only one afraid. Miles Standish and his men all wore full armor, and the captain firmly gripped his musket.

Chief Massasoit, invited to parley with the Elders, was offered brandy by Governor Carver to show his good faith.

Governor Carver motioned for Squanto to follow them into the Common House to act as interpreter. After several hours, Governor Carver announced a peace treaty between the Wampanoags and the colonists.

When Squanto glanced up and saw Merrie, the Indian grinned. "Just in time to help."

Merrie smiled. "What can I do?"

Squanto handed her a hoe. "Dig," he instructed. "I'll put the seed in each mound." His sharp eyes gleamed when he looked at her. "Time to plant corn," he said. "The leaves of the white oak are as big as a mouse's ear."

So that's how he knew, Merrie thought, as she took the hoe and dug a small hole. Squanto then dropped in a seed.

"Thanks to you," she said admiringly, gazing about at the cleared land, "we'll be able to plant this entire area." She looked at him warmly, thinking of all the things he'd taught them: how to plant corn, catch fish, trap beaver, and tap maple trees for sweet syrup. He was their guide, their interpreter, their friend. "Oh, Squanto," she burst out, touching his wrist, "we owe you so much."

"I like white people," Squanto said matter-of-factly. "I want to help you all I can." His smile broadened. "Now that there is peace with Chief Massasoit, I can help you more. I can even take you to the Wampanoags' village where I once lived."

"Would you?" she asked, her dark eyes sparkling.

"Yes, but remember: Plymouth is my home now!"

"And I'm glad it is," she said sincerely, "but be sure you know which side of the peace treaty to live up to!"

"My place is here." Squanto chuckled. "Enough planting and talking, Merrie." He grinned. "Come. I will show you how to get a delicacy for supper tonight."

What new thing was Squanto going to show her now, she wondered. She threw down her hoe.

At the sandy riverbank, Squanto tossed off his moccasins and waded into the water, squashing the soft mud with his feet. Suddenly a black snake surfaced, and Squanto quickly grabbed it. Holding up the squirming long shape, he shouted gleefully, "An eel!" His round face puckered into a wide grin. "Delicious to eat. Fat and sweet!" He went back to churning up the waters.

Merrie, big-eyed, watched the river as more eels thrashed to the surface.

"Kick off your shoes! See if you can catch one!"

Merrie threw back her head, laughing. "If

you can, *I* can!" She dashed behind a huckleberry bush, slipped off her shoes, and pulled off her black stockings.

In a minute she splashed into the icy water, feeling the soft cold mud ooze between her toes.

All at once a gleaming eel rose to the top, and although she grasped the sleek wiggler with both hands, it slipped away, plopping back into the water and disappearing into the mud.

Squanto caught one eel after another and efficiently thrust them into the bag dangling at his side.

Determined to catch at least one eel, Merrie hitched up her skirts to her bare knees and searched the water. Spying a thick squat eel, she plunged both hands beneath the surface, grabbing it by the tail. Laughing and squealing, she handed the wriggling ebony eel to Squanto. "I did it!" she crowed.

"Good!" he said, jamming the eel into his bulging sack. "Catch one more and we'll go!"

Reaching down in the murky waters, Merrie quickly grasped another eel, triumphantly holding it up in the air, but before she could give it to Squanto, she was shocked to hear her name.

"Merrie Courtland!" yelled a hoarse voice. "What do you think you're doing! Get out of there this instant!"

Merrie gasped at the sight of Oliver Loomis standing rigidly on the riverbank. With his hands on his hips and his black hat pulled down to his menacing brows, he glared at her.

At first she could only blankly stare at the tall black-dressed figure.

"Come out of there!" Loomis repeated furiously.

Not wanting to involve Squanto, Merrie motioned him away, and the Indian discreetly moved downstream.

Wading ashore, Merrie felt the mud suck at her feet, and wished the muck would hold her back. Instead, she gamely trudged forward. Her bubbling spirits had vanished.

Trembling, she stood before Master Loomis, who eyed her with disgust.

"Get your skirt down!" he snapped, anger almost choking him. "Put on your shoes and stockings and follow me back to Plymouth!"

Merrie, not knowing what to do with the squirming eel, threw it down.

The eel slithered over Master Loomis's heavy boot.

"Ugh!" he grunted, leaping back, and watching fearfully as the eel crawled toward the river.

Merrie couldn't speak to defend herself. Her throat was too tight. She had never seen Master Loomis so angry.

"A grown woman!" he said, his face crimson with rage. "You're nothing but a shameful vixen!" His angular features hardened. "The Council will know how to deal with the likes of you!" Merrie felt as if she were in her dream of drowning in icy water with Master Loomis's nasty words ringing in her ears.

Chapter Eleven

USING a tin dipper, Merrie skimmed off the floating grease globs that bubbled to the top of the iron kettle. For three days the bear and deer grease had been boiling until it became clear.

Mistress Patience had saved grease for months to dip candles, and Merrie was glad she'd chosen today for the disagreeable, smelly job. The hard work would help take her mind off the Council meeting this morning. Every time she tried to think of something else, her mind went right back to the Council and the men who would decide her future. Oliver Loomis was a leader in the Council, and he'd state a strong case against her.

The boiling tallow stung her eyes, and she bit her lip to keep the tears from brimming over. Would she be forced to leave Plymouth, she wondered.

Mistress Patience threw another log on the roaring fire, for candle-making required a blazing-hot fire. Patience didn't say a word, but Merrie thought she must know how afraid she was.

Merrie reached for one of the candle rods that dangled from two poles laid across chairbacks. Twisting the several wicks of entwined hemp before dipping it in the tallow, Merrie hesitantly asked, "Mistress Patience, c-could you put in a good word for me at the Council meeting?" Not daring to look at her, Merrie dipped the candle rod into the hot kettle and then hung it back on the pole to cool.

Mistress Patience silently took another group of half-finished hardened candles and dipped them for the fourth fattening coat. "No," she finally said. "Women do not appear before the Council, Merrie. You should know that."

"I guess I do," she answered glumly, "but my whole life is in the hands of the Council." Her spirits sank even lower. "And there's no one to speak for me." She sat at the table, her head in her hands.

"Merrie, remember Masters Carver, Bradford, Brewster, and Winslow are fair-minded men. I'm certain you won't need to leave Plymouth."

Despite the reassuring words and the raging fire, Merrie shivered. "But what if I do?" she asked in a small voice, unable to hide her inner misery.

Mistress Patience poured tea, handing Merrie a cup. "Don't borrow trouble," she said soothingly, but a slight frown darkened her face. "Drink this," she said gently. "You'll feel better."

Merrie took the cup gratefully, sipping the pungent hot drink, but although she tried to relax, nothing, not even Mistress Patience's sage tea, could make her terrible tenseness disappear.

All at once men's voices were heard, and Merrie leaped to her feet, upsetting the tea. The amber liquid soaked quickly into the newly sprinkled dirt floor.

"It doesn't matter," Mistress Patience said, patting Merrie's hand.

When the door opened, Merrie moved closer to Mistress Patience. Her eyes widened as Zack entered with William Bradford.

Solemn-faced, Elder Bradford cleared his throat, eyeing Merrie, then came right to the point. "Merrie Courtland, the Council will not punish you, although," he added sternly, "Oliver Loomis vehemently disapproved of your actions."

He glanced at Zack. "The Council, mainly due to Zachariah Gaines's eloquent defense, will give you another chance." A slight smile flickered across his craggy features. "Zachariah mentioned how you nursed the sick and saved Mistress Patience. Nonetheless," he continued firmly, running his fingers through his thick hair, "you did stow away, you shot a musket, and you fished for eels in bare feet.

From now on," he warned, "if we receive one more complaint, you'll be banished from Plymouth. Understood?"

Merrie nodded, staring at William Bradford, too tongue-tied to speak. The words "another chance" drummed in her ears, and she was so happy she wanted to jump to the rafters. But that wouldn't be good behavior, would it? William Bradford might be shocked.

"Well, what do you say to the Council's decision, Merrie?" Zack asked, laugh lines crinkling about his dark eyes.

Finding her voice, she stammered, "I-I don't know what to say." She turned to William Bradford. "I'll try to be what the Council expects of me. And I thank them from the bottom of my heart." To think the Council had gone against Oliver Loomis's recommendations! She knew if she made one mistake, Master Loomis would force her to leave. With a heavy heart, she wondered how she could live like a porcelain doll that would crack and break at the first misstep.

After William Bradford left, Zack took her arm. "Mind if I steal Merrie for a while, Mistress Patience?"

Patience, her round face wreathed in smiles, shooed them out with her apron. "Go, go. The candles need time to harden before we dip them again."

Merrie, grinning at Zack, snatched her cloak off the peg and wrapped it around her. She paused, then impulsively dashed back to

Patience and squeezed her hand. "Thanks," she said.

Patience, flustered, said, "Hurry or your young man won't wait," but she affectionately squeezed Merrie's hand in return.

Outside in the brisk March air, Merrie and Zack walked along the dirt lane with cabins on both sides, until they reached the clearing and the pine forest beyond.

Climbing a hill, they gazed east, out over the white-capped waves of the gray Atlantic. Zack took her hand in his, and she thrilled at his touch.

"Look," she said joyfully, pointing to a dipping sea gull. "I feel like that bird, floating and wheeling on the wind." She faced him, staring with grateful, glistening eyes. "Thanks to you, I can stay at Plymouth."

Zack smoothed back the blond curls that flew about her oval face. His dark eyes bored into hers, and they gazed at each other. Suddenly, he leaned down and lightly brushed his lips against her cheek.

"Oh, Zack," she said tremulously. "I've missed you." She lowered her long lashes. "It was a surprise to hear you had defended me before the Council." She looked at him, managing a tight little smile. "I thought you'd given up on me."

"And why would I do such a thing?" he asked, tightening his hold on her hand as they walked along the broad-topped hill.

Strolling to the other end of the hill, they watched the Jones River meandering like a huge blue snake below them. Eels! she thought with a shudder. Never again. From now on she'd be the perfect lady. Oliver Loomis wouldn't be able to find a single fault. With Zack at her side it would be much easier. After all, tomorrow was her birthday. She'd be sixteen — about time she grew up and acted like a lady.

For the rest of the afternoon Zack and Merrie sat together on a bluff overlooking Plymouth. Zack, his dark curly hair framing his strong, handsome face, sat on a rock with one booted leg bent. "This is beautiful land, isn't it?" he asked.

"Yes, oh, yes," she said lightheartedly, gazing at the melting snow on the tops of the fir trees. "I'm lucky to be here. If I were in London, I'd be getting married tomorrow."

"Tomorrow?" Zack asked incredulously, his heavy brows lifting.

"March 27th. My birthday," she said in a low, husky voice. "I'm lucky I'm not marrying Jeremiah Farmingham." She shot him a quick look. "You know, Zack, when you told me you planned on being a trapper, I didn't want to hear about it. It reminded me too much of Jeremiah, my trader fiancé." She smiled. "But I can see now that you're not at all like Jeremiah." She couldn't look at him but had to say what she felt. "I don't care what you do, Zack, as long as you're happy."

"But I do care what you do, Merrie," Zack said, tossing a pebble and watching it bounce down the cliffside. "I was afraid you'd be leaving for England. That you'd had enough of this colony, and . . ." he paused, giving her a sidelong glance, "the people around you."

Her heart jumped, and she yearned to tell him that the people around her were exactly the reason she wanted to stay. However, she didn't say anything. She was too afraid of breaking today's glorious spell. Also now she knew that Zack cared for her.

"So," he mused, "tomorrow the little 'stowaway girl' will be sixteen. How would you like to return to the river? We can't ice-skate, since the ice has melted, but we can walk along the bank — " he paused significantly " — and be together."

She remembered the tingle of his kiss. "I'd love to spend my birthday with you," she said, with shining eyes.

He laughed. "Your cheeks are redder than tulips, and your eyes are sparkling." He lifted her chin and ran his thumb over her cheek. The cold wind snapped around them, and Merrie's soft hair streamed out behind, her red cloak whipping about her. "I'd better get you back," Zack said at last, lightly, nodding toward the crimson sun deep in the west, "or Mistress Patience won't let you out of the cabin tomorrow."

Smiling, she touched his hand. "Nothing will ruin tomorrow. Not now," she said confidently, matching his long strides. "Not even

Master Loomis." She gave a short laugh. "He must be gnashing his teeth now over the Elders' decision."

"I'm sure he is," Zack said dryly, "but just don't cross him, Merrie. You should have heard how he raved to William Bradford. Fortunately, he couldn't persuade Bradford you were so evil. But next time, who knows?" He shrugged his lean shoulders. "I might not be there to plead your case." He grinned at her. "So, Merrie, try to be good."

"I promise," she said quickly, not wanting to think about Oliver Loomis! Not on such a joyful day! "And how are you and Miles Standish getting along?" she asked.

Zack's broad mocking smile made her smile, too. It was as if he knew she had deliberately changed the subject.

"Miles hasn't been so cantankerous lately," he said. "In fact, he's been almost cheerful."

"And why is that?"

"Haven't you heard?" Zack said, with an amused glint in his eyes. "He's romancing a few widows, and I wouldn't be surprised if he doesn't get remarried this spring."

Astonished, she said, "But Rose has only been dead two months." How fast romances blossomed between widowers and widows after a winter of deaths, she thought. No one wanted to be alone in this harsh land. Even Susanna White with her new son, Peregrine, was being courted by several men. And William, her husband, had been dead less than two months. But Merrie had her own blossoming romance and couldn't worry about anyone else's.

That night her dreams were of Zack, and not once did Oliver Loomis trouble her sleep.

The next morning Merrie rose at dawn to help Mistress Patience spin and card wool. But all the while her thoughts were on her birthday. Today she was sixteen! Sixteen and in love!

Mistress Patience, in a neat dark dress with a white collar, white apron, and white cap, stood quietly watching Merrie. The only ornament on her dress was a rope around her waist containing a set of jangling keys. "Today is your day, Merrie," she said. "I want you out of the house so I can cook a special dinner. By the way, why don't you ask Zack for supper?"

Merrie could have hugged her. Sometimes Mistress Patience was very understanding.

"Your gift is by the fireplace," Mistress Patience said.

Merrie's eyes widened when she glimpsed a pair of black boots on the hearth. Dashing over, she picked one up, and ran her fingers over the soft leather and fine workmanship.

"I traded Daniel's boots for a pair of boy's boots from William Mullins's stock," Patience explained simply. "The way you tramp in the woods and along the beach, Merrie, I thought you'd appreciate boots more than slippers."

Merrie knew that William Mullins had brought one hundred twenty-six pairs of shoes and thirteen pairs of boots aboard the *Mayflower* and before he died had willed the entire shipment to the company with his daughter, Priscilla, in charge. Poor Priscilla Mullins, Merrie thought. She not only had lost both parents to the "general sickness," but her brother as well. Merrie tried to dismiss the dismal memory as she kicked off her threadbare shoes and pulled on the shiny boots.

The fit was perfect! "Thank you, Mistress Patience," she said, running and hugging her. "I couldn't have received a better present!" Patience was like the mother she'd never known, and although it had taken them quite a while to get to know each other, a strong bond now existed between them.

"Run along, Merrie," Patience said gently, her clear blue eyes suspiciously moist. "I have work to do."

Merrie happily put on her new dress and from beneath the bed pulled out her small box of treasures — a Greek myth book and a red ribbon. Whirling about in her gingham dress, Merrie felt the flared skirt fly out, above the flounce of her white petticoats. She knew exactly what she'd do with her free day. She'd leave Milton's *Paradise Lost* on the shelf and again read all sixteen myths by the seashore.

Waving good-bye to Patience, she hurried down to the white sand and the sun. She felt beautiful in her new dress, and, when she was out of sight of the settlement, she took out the crimson satin ribbon, her one reminder of home, that she'd been saving for a special occasion.

Sixteen, she reminded herself, as she tied back her hair with the wide ribbon. The bow, huge and scarlet, accented the tiny red flowers in her dark dress, and the pretty tie rested on the nape of her neck, sticking out like two triangular sails. She hugged herself when she thought of later this afternoon when Zack would be waiting for her.

Spreading her cloak on the glistening white sand, she let the warm spring sun beat down on her. She opened her book to the tale of Icarus and Daedalus. The young Greek, Icarus, had defied the sun, flying too close with his wax wings. The wings had melted and he had fallen into the sea, drowning. A shadow darkened her face. Could things be too wonderful? She slammed shut her book, not wanting to read or think about tragedy. Instead, she watched the pounding waves crashing and rushing against the shore.

Her dark thoughts forgotten, she suddenly jumped up and sprinted toward the water. She wished she could pull off her boots and splash in the waves, but yesterday was too fresh in her mind. Nonetheless, she twirled about, exuberant and wildly happy. She ran along the beach and stopped to spin around. The sailors' Anchor Song echoed in her head, and as she danced she sang:

"Heigh ho-o-o-o-, up she rises
Heigh ho-o-o-o, up she rises, early in the
    morning.
Whachu gonna do-o-o with a drunken
    sailor
Put him in the longboat and — "

"Stop!" thundered Master Bradford's voice.

Merrie spun about. There stood Master Loomis and Master Bradford. Each man held a musket and had a bag of ducks slung over his shoulder. They glowered at her.

Merrie stared, unable to breathe because her throat was as hot and dry as the sand on which she stood.

All at once Master Loomis snatched up her precious myth book, ripped it in two, and flung the fluttering pages into the ocean. Then, his cold eyes fastened on her as he slowly spat out the words: "Dancing! Singing a sailors' song! Reading Greek stories! And with a red ribbon in her loose hair!" His eyes glittered with malice as he confronted William Bradford. "Have you seen enough, Master Bradford?"

Master Bradford's usually pleasant face was white with anger. "How dare you mock our decision to give you another chance?" he said, his tone ominously calm. "Follow me, Merrie Courtland!"

But Merrie was rooted to the spot. Her legs had turned to stone, and her heart to granite!

Chapter Twelve

MERRIE, with lowered head and downcast eyes, waited outside the Common House. She swallowed with difficulty when she remembered how happy she'd been that afternoon. Had it been only one short hour ago that she'd been dancing on the beach? This time she had no illusions about whether the Elders would punish her or not. But she could only guess what her sentence would be.

She didn't have long to wait.

Governor Carver, his long face even longer, confronted her. "Merrie Courtland, the Council will give you two choices. You will either spend one week in the stocks or be exiled from Plymouth a week." His voice was grave as he peered at her beneath shaggy brows. "Which will it be?"

Merrie gulped, unable to force any words past her dry lips, trying to think of her choices. If her hands and feet were locked

in wooden stocks, she'd be held up to ridicule
for a week. The image was not a pleasant
one. It would hurt Zack and Patience, too.
On the other hand, if she wandered in the
woods for a week, she would be out of sight,
and her friends wouldn't be forced to share
her shame. Taking a shaky breath, she faced
Governor Carver and said in a trembling
voice, "I'll leave Plymouth."

In the background she glimpsed the smirk
on Oliver Loomis's thin face. His eyes were
as gray and hard as a stone.

"Very well," John Carver said levelly. "In
one hour you'll be gone from the colony!" He
turned, going back into the Common House.

One hour, she thought. She stood rigidly
in the sun, and a slight tremor ran up her
spine. What would Zack say, she wondered
in despair. Where is he now? She gave a
small sigh. Even if he'd been here, he couldn't
have saved her this time.

All at once the door opened, and the Elders,
shouldering hoes and shovels on their way
to the fields, filed silently past her. No one
glanced at her. She looked at each one with
misty eyes. Didn't they know it was her
birthday? Why are you doing this? she
wanted to shout. I didn't harm anyone!
Pilgrims and their narrow customs, she
thought sourly. Well, I'm glad I'm not one of
you!

But her heart ached. How many times had
she admired their grit and determination.
They had goals and principles and stuck to

them. Slowly, she removed the red ribbon from her hair. She should braid her mass of curls and coil them in a topknot, but as she walked away, staring with unseeing eyes at the dirt path, she wondered why she should bother. It wasn't only her myth book that had been destroyed, but her happy spirit, as well. Tears blinded her. And tonight was to have been so special. A delicious dinner with the two people she loved. A tear trickled down her cheek. One hour, she thought with panic, to leave Plymouth. Stumbling, she broke into a run.

Reaching the cabin, she burst in, only to find the room empty. A large chicken, crispy brown, was on the spit, and the hasty pudding simmered in an iron kettle. Suddenly, she remembered Patience was spending the afternoon at Mary Brewster's quilting bee.

Quickly, Merrie dipped out the corn, and while it cooled, she changed clothes. She'd need the warmth of her red wool dress, and the corn was the most nourishing food she could take. She'd learned this from Squanto. Corn would keep her alive for at least three days, and surely she could survive for the rest of the week. She wished she could tell Zack and Patience good-bye, but they'd hear the news of her banishment soon enough.

Flinging her cloak over her arm and carrying her food cache, she left, feeling miserable and closing the door behind her. Zack had jokingly warned her "to be good," and now her wild ways had caught up with her. She couldn't be good for even one day! Zack would be disappointed and wouldn't want a "stowaway girl" who couldn't learn to behave! Oh, Zack, she thought miserably, I've failed you.

What was wrong with her? Why had she danced and sung? Why had she let her hair fly? Why had she worn a red ribbon? Reaching the hilltop graves, she gazed down at Plymouth for one last time. The small cabins huddled together, and the newly planted fenced gardens with boards to separate the vegetables was a lovely sight in the waning sun. Would she ever see it again? She flung her cloak about her and stared into the woods. Or would a wild animal devour her?

Hurriedly, she headed for the river and the cliffs where she and Zack had been. Had it been only yesterday when he had kissed her?

For hours she walked, but the lengthening evening shadows that spread across the forest meant she must make camp soon. At last she came to a sheltered rocky alcove where she gathered twigs and branches for a fire. She was glad she'd remembered the tinderbox. Taking out the charred shreds of linen and the chunks of flint and steel, she lit the fire. With her knees up to her chin, she sadly watched the orange blaze, feeling lonely and scared. So this is the end of my perfect birthday, she thought bitterly.

A wolf howled, and her arms tightened

about her knees. The sack of corn was beside her, but she couldn't eat. Finally she lay down, pulling her fur-lined cloak to her chin, and closed her eyes, but she was too upset to sleep.

The endless night finally grayed into a morning fog that hung over the river like wispy smoke. A fine drizzle fell on her face, and she trembled. Which way should she go? In despair, she rose, staring at the dripping glistening trees and the blue-black river. A cold damp wind tumbled her hair, and she rubbed her arms. She wasn't hungry, but to keep up her strength, she ate a bite of corn and set off.

The rain grew heavy and pelted against her face. She staggered blindly ahead, thinking of the cozy fireplace in the cabin. Wet and bedraggled, she almost whimpered aloud as she tramped through the soggy forest. Silently, she blessed Patience for her birthday boots. At least her feet were dry.

All day she moved deeper into the woods, wending her way between the white birch and maple trees until she lost all sense of direction. The cloudy overcast sky matched her dark mood as she slogged ahead. Tears welled up in her eyes, spilling over. On and off, she had cried all day, unable to stop. Now, however, she was determined to forge ahead and quit feeling sorry for herself.

By evening she was desperate to get out of the cold rain, which had now slowed to a steady patter. The forest gave way to rocky cliffs, and a black opening yawned ahead. A cave, she thought, with a surge of hope. She broke into a run.

Scrambling up a steep incline, she approached the cave. Carefully, she pushed aside tangled vines and brush, and warily stepped inside. A rustle stopped her. Rigid with fear, she couldn't move a step further. Were bats about to swoop down on her? Or did a bear stir, awakening from his winter's nap?

When her eyes became accustomed to the gloom, she peered in the dark corners. Then, convinced she was alone, she sank to the stone floor, exhausted. By the remains of a fire she knew someone else had stayed here. Indians perhaps? But she was too tired and too filled with anguish to care. To think this was only the second day of her exile, and already she was so defeated that she didn't care if she lived or died. She closed her eyes, too utterly miserable even to cry.

By the fourth day, Merrie felt a little better. In three days she'd be able to return to Plymouth. The day before, however, she had eaten the last of the corn, and her stomach rumbled with sharp hunger pangs. She must find food!

Emerging from the cave, she looked about, wondering where to go. The forest loomed ahead, but she could tell by the rising sun that east was to her left. This morning, she thought, I'll search for nuts or early spring berries.

For hours Merrie hunted for food, but no berries were left on the bushes, and when she poked through the sodden leaves, hoping for at least a ground nut, she was hopelessly disappointed.

Squinting at the blue sky, she could tell by the overhead sun that it was noon. Perhaps she should head for the river and catch a fish. The memory of Squanto, bringing the colonists fish, crabs, oysters, clams, and lobster came floating back. How good the boiled lobster had tasted! For a moment she swayed, dizzy from hunger. Where was the river? The woods were so thick she didn't know where to turn.

Hesitantly, she started in the direction of the pin oaks, but the woods only became darker and thicker. She licked her dry lips and tried to swallow. She was thirsty, too. She had to reach the river and get water.

Plunging on, she ignored the branches and brambles that tore at her skirts and scratched her face. A spurt of panic raced through her when she thought she might not find the river. If she didn't, she'd die of hunger and thirst!

Suddenly she froze. A crashing noise echoed throughout the forest. Her heartbeat pounded in her ears as she strained to see into the thick underbrush. What new terror was coming after her? A grizzly bear? A wolf? An Indian hunting party?

All at once a large white-tailed deer loomed before her. Merrie held her breath. For a moment the buck and Merrie stared at each other. Finally, with a toss of his antlers, the deer bounded in the opposite direction and disappeared among the pines.

Gasping with relief, Merrie sank down on the soft pine needles to catch her breath. But hunger soon forced her to her feet. Wearily, she lurched forward, struggling through the brambles. Once thorns snagged her sleeve, ripping it. Fleetingly, she thought of her red dress and how torn and tattered it had become.

Coming to a clearing, she saw below her a patch of blue glinting in the sunlight. The river! Madly, she rushed toward it, half slipping, half falling down the hillside.

At the river's edge, she plunged into the water and scooped up a handful of water. It was the best thing she'd ever tasted! She dashed the water against her face and felt refreshingly revived. Standing in ankle-deep water, she saw a fish leap into the air and splash back into the river. Would it be possible to catch a fish with her bare hands as she'd seen Squanto do many times?

Wading farther out, she looked down into the clear water. Too late she glimpsed the beaver trap hidden beneath the water. Steel jaws clamped shut on her ankle, and excruciating shock waves of pain shot through her body.

Chapter Thirteen

MERRIE sank down on one knee, water swirling around her, and desperately tried to pry the beaver trap open. Time and again she pulled on the iron claws, but they held firm. Her fingers, stiff and frozen, were rapidly becoming numb with cold. The metal teeth were too strong. It was useless. Sheer black fright washed over her. What would happen to her alone with night coming on?

Panic-stricken, she searched her memory. How did a beaver trap work? Squanto had shown her. Beaver traps, he had explained, were always set in shallow water, for even though beavers were aquatic, they easily drowned. If she hadn't been so eager for a drink, she'd have seen the danger.

Oh, how her ankle throbbed. She had to get free! Frantically, she again reached down, clawing at the saw-toothed jaws. But it was hopeless. She was caught.

Gazing up and down the riverbank, she watched for some movement, some sign of life. Where there were traps there had to be trappers.

The rapidly setting afternoon sun alarmed her. How could she survive a night in the cold river? "Help!" she called, but her hoarse voice could barely be heard above the rushing stream. "Someone, please!" Her head was light, and she was afraid of fainting, but she fought to hang on to her fragile control. She knew she had to keep her wits about her if she hoped to stay alive.

She moaned. She might struggle to keep awake, but what good would it do her if no one found her in this vast wilderness? Yielding to her fear, she let tears of despair roll down her cheeks. She felt the color drain from her face and dug her nails into her wrist, praying she wouldn't pass out. She stopped crying and, with tears still trembling on her lashes, thought, I won't drown in eight inches of water! I won't!

All at once she heard something crashing through the woods. Keeping her eyes closed, she wondered if wolves could swim. Then, in spite of her fear, she looked toward the sound. She was astonished to see an Indian girl running toward the river. Relieved, Merrie cried aloud, "Help me!" She reached out to her rescuer. "My foot is caught," she whimpered.

The Indian girl quickly waded into the water, and with an experienced, powerful effort forced the trap's blades apart. Merrie jerked her foot out, wavered, and would have fallen if she hadn't grabbed the girl's shoulder.

Merrie's rescuer rose to her feet, her straight black hair falling softly about her lovely, sympathetic face. She had gentle black eyes. "I am Little Fawn of the Wampanoags," she said. "Come." She motioned. "We'll go to the shore, and I'll look at your ankle."

Merrie wasn't surprised Little Fawn spoke English, after hearing Samoset and Squanto. Merrie waded a few steps but collapsed in the water, churning up the sandy bottom.

The Indian girl grabbed her hand and pulled her up, then placed Merrie's arm around her shoulder.

"I'm so glad to see you," Merrie said in a halting, anguished voice as she limped to shore, supported by the Indian girl.

Little Fawn helped her sit down on the bank, and Merrie tenderly touched her swollen, bleeding ankle.

"I will make your ankle well," Little Fawn said. "Wait here." In one fluid motion, she rose and sprinted toward the trees.

Merrie lay on the shore, one arm flung over her eyes. The agonizing pulse in her leg was unbearable. Soon, however, she drifted off into a misty dreamlike state.

When Little Fawn returned, she carried sprigs of wild daisies. Silently and efficiently she spread the flowers on a rock and then, with a stone, mashed them to a pulp. From her leather bag, she pulled forth a vial of animal fat, then mixed the two together until it was a smooth paste. Merrie turned her head and watched with interest. If this new concoction worked, she'd use it at Plymouth. Plymouth, she thought with a pang, and struggled to sit up.

Little Fawn examined Merrie's ankle, then bathed the torn flesh in clear water. Next she carefully smeared the yellow medicine over the cuts. "This hurts," she said knowingly.

Merrie winced. "It does," she agreed, bracing herself against the pain.

When she'd finished, Little Fawn covered the ankle with birchbark and nodded. "Ankle better in few days. Can you walk now?" She offered Merrie her hand.

"I-I don't know," Merrie said hesitantly, taking Little Fawn's hand. Standing, she hobbled about on one foot, but when she put her weight on her lacerated ankle, she cried out with pain and almost fell to the ground. Fire arrows flew through her leg. "No, no, I can't," Merrie groaned, massaging her shinbone. "You go ahead, Little Fawn. I'll be all right."

"Only to Sowans, Chief Massasoit's village," Little Fawn said. "I will return with my brother and father before night." Her black eyes stared at Merrie with gentle concern as she unfastened her leather fringed shawl and draped it around Merrie's shoulders. "You sleep while the medicine work," she ordered.

"Th-thank you, Little Fawn." Merrie felt her senses deserting her. Comets and stars whirled together, and she gratefully fell back on the new grass to rest. Already the herb mixture was having a soothing effect on her hurt ankle.

Dusk settled over the area, and a loon's cry was heard on the quiet air.

Drifting in and out of consciousness, she hoped Little Fawn wouldn't forget about her. She didn't know how long it was before she saw Little Fawn step out of the woods, leading a young boy and a straight-backed un-smiling warrior toward her.

Little Fawn hurried to Merrie's side. "I brought Black Eagle, my father, and my brother, Fierce Falcon. We will bring you to our village."

"Who are you?" the young boy questioned, pulling a litter forward.

"I'm Merrie Courtland from Plymouth," she answered, managing a small smile.

"We do not need the carrying bed," Black Eagle said to his son. "I can carry her. She is lighter than you, Fierce Falcon."

"I am ten summers," Fierce Falcon boasted. "I am a warrior."

"In few years," Black Eagle said dryly. He looked at Merrie through narrowed eyes. "Why are you in the woods alone?" he asked suspiciously.

Merrie's smile faded, and her palms grew

sweaty. She didn't know what to say. If Black Eagle knew she was an outcast, he might not help her. "I-I lost my way," she lied, almost choking on the words.

Black Eagle grunted. "Come, I'll carry you to Sowans." With one deft motion, he lifted her in his sinewy arms.

"Shall I run to Plymouth and tell them we have Merrie?" Fierce Falcon asked eagerly.

Merrie, resting her head on Black Eagle's shoulder, jerked to attention. "No, no," she said quickly. "I-I will soon see everyone there." She dared not look at Black Eagle.

At Sowans Merrie was amazed at the long rectangular wigwams, even longer than the *Mayflower*'s deck. The dwellings were clustered about a large open space and scattered campfires blazed before each one. Hundreds of Indians came out to view the strange white girl. Merrie hid her face in the hollow of Black Eagle's shoulder. She was embarrassed to be such a spectacle.

As Black Eagle carried Merrie to a huge wigwam with a wooden beaver carved over the entrance, she lifted her head and stared into the eyes of an attractive woman who looked curiously back at Merrie. The squaw wore an elaborate beaded headband and a shell belt that cinched in a small waist. Black Eagle ducked his head beneath the low-hanging deerskin covering and went inside. "Singing Wren," he called to the pretty woman, "come in and take care of this sick girl." Carefully he put Merrie down on a bunk lined with furs.

"I'll bring steamed clams, my husband," Singing Wren said and smiled at Merrie. "Little Fawn told me about your foot. My daughter is a good medicine woman," Singing Wren said proudly, eyes sparkling. "Her mother teaches her."

"Hurry, wife," Black Eagle barked, but his iron demeanor softened when he glanced at her.

"Yes, my husband," Singing Wren answered pleasantly, her round face bursting into a sunny smile. "My husband is not so gruff as he seems," she said lightly to Merrie and hurried away to the cooking fire.

Merrie's mouth watered when she smelled clams, oysters, and mussels. She hadn't had food for days. How wonderfully lucky she was to be here! The fox fur, the warmth of the fire, and the cooking odors all lulled her into a drowsy feeling of contentment. She stared at the poles, covered with woven mats, that sprang inward and formed supporting arches for the wigwam's hickory bark frame. Lazy swirls of smoke escaped through the roof-hole. The orange fire dimly lit the large storage baskets, dried yellow squash, ears of corn, and salted fish that hung from the ceiling.

Singing Wren handed Merrie a bowl of clams and mussels that had been steaming over hot rocks. "Eat," she commanded.

Merrie gulped down the tasty clams. Never

had food tasted this marvelous. When she'd eaten her fill, she sank back on the furs and fell into a deep sleep.

She awakened to find bright sun streaming through the roof opening and the wigwam teeming with activity.

Merrie turned her head and felt fur soft against her cheek. Little Fawn, sitting nearby, was shaking a bark tray of wild rice back and forth. Winnowing out any bad kernels, she poured the good rice grains into a limp basket, shaped more like a bag, and fastened it to the ceiling hook.

Merrie enjoyed watching the beautiful dark girl who was so intent on her task. "Good morning," Merrie finally said, sitting up carefully and smiling.

Little Fawn looked up, returning Merrie's smile. "How do you feel?" she asked.

"Much better," Merrie said.

"Hungry?"

"Yes," Merrie answered. "I didn't think I'd ever be hungry again after all the seafood I had last night."

Little Fawn laughed, a low throaty sound that warmed Merrie. "Two nights ago."

"Two nights?" Merrie repeated, dumbfounded.

"Yes," Little Fawn said. "You slept like the spirit of the dead."

"Is today Monday?" Merrie asked incredulously.

"Two days," Little Fawn repeated, rising

gracefully and going to the center of the wigwam's cooking fire. An iron pot rested on a slanting forked pole that jutted over the flames. She dished up a bowl of boiled corn.

Monday, Merrie thought with dismay. A week ago she'd been expelled from Plymouth.

When Little Fawn brought her the steaming bowl of corn, she ate it, but her appetite had diminished. She kept thinking of Plymouth. Did the Elders expect her to return? Or did they want her to find a new home — far away from Plymouth? She pushed the bowl aside, unable to eat anymore.

"How is your ankle?" Little Fawn asked, throwing back the bearskin and tenderly touching the swelling.

"Wh-what?" Merrie asked, scarcely thinking of her wound. "Oh," she said, "it's stiff and sore — but better."

Little Fawn poured a small amount of maple syrup into a cup and mixed it with water. "Drink this to give you strength."

Merrie downed the sweet maple syrup. "Delicious," she murmured, but wished she were alone. She had to decide if she'd leave for Plymouth today.

Chapter Fourteen

As Merrie lay on her bed, worried about Plymouth, someone pulled back the door flap. Astonished, Merrie watched big-eyed as Chief Massasoit entered the wigwam with Black Eagle behind.

Merrie sat up, a twinge of pain running along her ankle. The grand sachem of the Wampanoags, looking resplendent in a vest decorated with porcupine quills and leather long-fringed trousers, strode over to her bed.

Hastily, Merrie smoothed back her tumbled hair and waited for him to speak. She hoped she wouldn't be asked to leave Sowans. Not yet! Even though she had stayed away from Plymouth the allotted seven days, she wasn't ready to face the Elders just yet.

"Chief Massasoit," she said, finding her voice, "I am honored."

Quizzically, the chief looked at Black Eagle,

who lost no time in interpreting her words for him.

She smiled, struggling to stand, but the chief motioned, and Black Eagle pushed her back on the bed. The chief spoke, his voice deep and melodious. Squanto had taught Merrie a few Indian words, but she couldn't understand Chief Massasoit's rapid speech. She glanced with puzzlement at Black Eagle.

Black Eagle again intervened and smoothly translated, "Chief Massasoit says he is glad you here. We will escort you back to Plymouth today."

Panic-stricken, Merrie glanced at Black Eagle. He returned her glance with dark eyes that glittered like black glass. She quickly pointed to herself and then the bed, willing the chief to comprehend. "I want to stay here for two days," she said in a clear voice.

Black Eagle's eyes narrowed, and he kept them on her face as he translated her words. His look was speculative, and Merrie wondered if he had guessed her guilty secret.

Surprised, Chief Massasoit nodded and spoke with gestures.

"He says you're welcome," Black Eagle said. "But he wonders why you wish not to go back." A small smile flickered over his lips. "I will tell him you were lost in woods. True?"

Merrie looked down at her clasped hands. Her heart hammered painfully. She must tell these two imposing Indians the truth, for when she returned to Plymouth, they'd soon discover why she had been sent away. She licked her lips. "I-I wasn't lost in the woods," she said in a barely audible voice. "I was forced to leave Plymouth."

Black Eagle stared unsurprisedly at her, as if he'd known all along she'd lied to him. "And why did the settlers turn you away?"

For a moment she said nothing. How could she explain she had been caught reading a bad book? How would they understand, with bright feathers in their hair, that she'd dared wear her hair loose and tied with a red ribbon? How could she explain she'd been dancing and singing the wrong song?

At last Merrie whispered, "I-I went against their customs." She frantically searched for a way to make him understand. She decided to tell them what she'd done.

When she'd completed the events leading up to her banishment, Black Eagle's impassive face suddenly broke into a smile. He repeated her words to Chief Massasoit, stopping once to reach over and lift a strand of her long hair and to pluck a red feather from his head and stick it behind Merrie's ear.

At the end of Black Eagle's explanation, the chief guffawed and began to talk animatedly in his own language.

Black Eagle translated in an amused tone. "Chief say ways of Pilgrims strange ways. When Samoset first visited Plymouth, he wore leather loincloth. The Pilgrims rushed to cover him with a coat." Black Eagle grinned. "They said Samoset was not decent. The chief understands why you are here." His eyes warmed. "I understand, too. You may stay with us as long as you want."

Her eyes sparkled, and her face lit up. "Two days and then I must go back." She knew she'd have to face the Elders sooner or later, so why delay? Besides, Zack, Luke, and Mistress Patience would be worried. But she wanted to stay two more days at Sowans. It would give her time to recuperate — and to think.

The chief and Black Eagle, lifting their hands in a good-natured salute, left.

That evening Little Fawn and Merrie walked around the open ceremonial space. Merrie limped, but with Little Fawn's arm about her waist she was walking much better, and her ankle no longer throbbed with pain. Perhaps the fresh herb salve that Little Fawn had applied to her wound had helped, too.

She and Little Fawn walked to a big oak on the edge of camp and sat under the new-leafed branches.

Little Fawn stretched out her long lithe legs and Merrie noticed her exquisite moccasins. "Little Fawn," she said, "your moccasins are beautiful."

Little Fawn smiled appreciatively. "I collect shells and beads and sew them on myself," she said. "My mother helps me stretch and tan deerskin, though."

"I like Singing Wren," Merrie said wistfully. "You're lucky to have such a mother." Little Fawn was so close to her mother, she thought. Not that she didn't love Mistress Patience. But sometimes she wondered if Mistress Patience loved her.

"You know, Little Fawn," Merrie said, "you saved my life." She touched Little Fawn's slender wrist. "I'm grateful," she said simply, "and want to give you a gift." She pulled from her pocket her crumpled red ribbon. "But this is all I have." She pressed the satin strip in Little Fawn's hand. "Would you take this, please?"

Little Fawn took the ribbon, holding it up and letting it flutter in the breeze. How she'd love to give Little Fawn something fabulous from her possessions at home in London. Little Fawn would have loved her dressing table mirror. The carved silver back, studded with bits of jade, was stunning.

"The ribbon is lovely," Little Fawn said. "I like it." With a quick motion she tied the crimson bow about her neck, giving her leather dress a splash of color.

Merrie felt a warm glow. Suddenly she asked impulsively, "Will you come to Plymouth to visit me?"

Little Fawn nodded eagerly. "I would like to see you again. I would like to learn about white people. I will come soon."

"And I like to learn about the Indians," Merrie said, laughing.

"We will make a pact," Little Fawn said, her face lighting up in a smile. She unsheathed a knife from her belt. "We will become blood sisters."

Merrie took a deep breath of amazement. "I'd like that," she said, a slight tremor in her voice.

The knife's blade glinted in the sun. With a clean stroke, Little Fawn made a tiny cut on her thumb and on Merrie's. Little Fawn pressed her thumb against Merrie's. "I pledge to always be your sister, Merrie."

"And I pledge to be your sister, Little Fawn, forever and ever," Merrie said huskily.

The two girls gazed warmly at each other, then impetuously, Merrie embraced Little Fawn. For a moment they clung to each other. Merrie was filled with love. At last, Merrie thought, she'd found the girl friend she'd yearned for. Her banishment had brought a wonderful friend — a sister.

Breaking away, Merrie laughed softly. "I hope you don't have to mix more wild daisies to heal this cut," she said impishly.

"No, no," Little Fawn said. "It heals quickly." She sucked at her own thumb. "Come, my sister. We will go back now. It is not good to get your ankle cold."

But it was April, and the soft breeze warmed Merrie. "I'm not cold, Little Fawn," she said. "I could stay here forever."

Little Fawn chuckled. "Me, too. But look!" She pointed at a file of Indian boys heading for the village with long strings of fish. "We have work to do."

"Work?" Merrie asked, wrinkling her nose. "What kind of work?"

"Cleaning and drying fish."

Merrie groaned. "Indian women work as hard as Pilgrim women." But she didn't mind. "Lead on, Little Fawn. I'll hobble behind and test my ankle."

When they arrived at the long tables used for cleaning fish, Little Fawn left Merrie and hurried to Fierce Falcon's side. The little boy, frowning, had disgustedly flung his fish on the table and walked to the campfire. He stood alone, rubbing his arms and staring at the flames. Little Fawn hurried to him. She leaned down, speaking quietly. Fierce Falcon listened attentively.

Merrie limped toward the two, and when she joined them, she was surprised to see Fierce Falcon's bottom lip quiver, almost as if he were about to cry. But Indian boys didn't cry — especially when they were as old as ten summers.

"What's wrong?" Merrie asked, glancing from Little Fawn to Fierce Falcon.

Little Fawn, her hands on her brother's shoulders, shook her head. "The children hate it when the men poison the stream to kill fish."

"Why?" Merrie asked.

"Because they must wade in to gather the dead fish."

"And the water is poisoned?"

"Yes, with Indian turnip."

"Indian turnip?" Merrie repeated, confused.

"The white people call Indian turnip jack-in-the-pulpit."

Fierce Falcon, his round face glowering, said, "The salmon float to the top, and we go in and get them."

Merrie eyed the dead salmon on the cleaning table. "Are the fish safe to eat?" she asked.

"Yes," Little Fawn answered, "the poison does not hurt people."

"But look what it's done to Fierce Falcon's arms," Merrie said in dismay.

Fierce Falcon scratched his elbow. "It makes a rash," he said.

"Why, that's terrible," Merrie said indignantly. "Does it irritate all children's skin this way?"

"Yes," Little Fawn said with a sigh. "I remember the redness all over my body when I was sent into river. When I was thirteen summers, though, I became woman and did not have to do this children's task again."

Fierce Falcon nodded. "I will soon be a warrior. Then I don't have to gather dead fish ever again."

Merrie shuddered, sharing the little boy's dread of such a painfully disagreeable job.

Little Fawn turned to Merrie. "Now it is time to clean the fish." She gave Fierce

Falcon's shoulder a playful squeeze. "You go clean yourself in fresh water and join Father for bow and arrow target practice."

Merrie walked over to the dozens of large salmon, rolled up her sleeves, took the sharp knife Little Fawn offered her, and began to scale the first fish.

On April 3rd, with the sky overcast, Merrie was ready to go back to Plymouth. Her heart beat slowly and heavily. She hated to leave. Although she was eager to see Zack, she dreaded how she'd be received.

She had dressed carefully. Her new moccasins, given to her by Little Fawn and Singing Wren, fit well and were beautifully stitched. They were so soft and pliable that it felt almost as if she were barefoot, especially after wearing heavy boots. Proudly, she fingered the elk tooth necklace that Little Fawn had taken from her neck and placed around hers. Would Oliver Loomis object to that?

As Merrie lingered at the entrance, gazing at the gray clouds, Singing Wren came and shyly touched Merrie's neatly braided hair. "You are like the sun that brightens our lives," she said, smiling. "You are a good girl, Merrie. You help us. I feel love when I look at you." She hugged her, and Merrie held Singing Wren tight.

"You are like my second daughter," Singing Wren continued, looking at her with shining black eyes.

"I *am* your daughter," Merrie said, looking

at the tiny thumb scar. It was true. Little
Fawn was her sister, and Singing Wren was
her mother.

"We must go now," Little Fawn urged,
tugging at Merrie's sleeve. "Father waits."

Gently Merrie pulled away. "I'll never forget your kindness to me, Singing Wren."
Hastily she went outside.

"Ready?" Black Eagle asked.

"I'm ready," Merrie responded with wet
eyes.

"Ah," Black Eagle said. "We must wait!
Here comes Chief Massasoit."

"To say good-bye," Little Fawn added.

Merrie was pleased and surprised that the
grand sachem himself had thought enough of
her to tell her good-bye.

The chief stood before Merrie, placing his
hand on the top of her thick hair, and spoke.

Black Eagle translated: "We need more
white people like you. You throw the hoop
and pole with Fierce Falcon. You do bead-
work with Little Fawn. You clean fish."

"Tell the chief I feel like a Wampanoag,"
she said.

The chief spoke again. "You are a good
Wampanoag."

Black Eagle translated and said, "I agree
with the chief. Now we must go."

But she stood staring at Chief Massasoit.
Everyone had given her so much, and she had
nothing to give in return. Oh, a red ribbon,
but what was that! She knew she might never
see the chief again. Suddenly she dashed

forward and threw her arms about his waist and hugged him.

Stunned, the chief stepped back.

Merrie, flustered, couldn't meet his eyes.

Then the Indian leader spoke in a clear voice. His face was dark and sober.

Merrie felt a stain of red warm her cheeks. She had been a silly little girl to give in to such an outburst. What must the chief think of her?

Black Eagle cleared his throat and said, "The chief says you are like an ambassador to the Indians. Like Squanto is an ambassador to white people."

Merrie looked up. Did she detect a glint of humor in the chief's eyes? His words meant more to her than all the gifts she'd received. She wanted to dash forward again and express her love. But she restrained herself and solemnly bowed her head instead.

With tears glistening in her eyes, she quickly turned and followed Little Fawn and Black Eagle. Her moccasined feet didn't make a sound as she stepped on the damp dead leaves from winter.

How she wished she could find the same love in Plymouth as she'd found at Sowans. She felt a hard knot form in her stomach. She knew the colonists would never offer such love and respect.

Chapter
Fifteen

LITTLE Fawn and Black Eagle left Merrie at the fort on the outskirts of Plymouth late in the afternoon and went back to their village. Merrie drew a deep breath, jutted out her chin, and marched resolutely down the dirt path into Plymouth.

Most of the men were in the fields, but the women were outside. Some were baking bread in the clay ovens, others were airing bedding and washing clothes. Merrie felt her cheeks burn at the surprised stares. No one came to her and said they were glad she was back.

Coming to Mistress Patience's cabin, Merrie paused before the closed door, braced herself, then opened it.

Mistress Patience, her white-capped head bent, was slowly turning the spit over the fireplace. A roast duck dripped sizzling fat into the fire. Merrie's heart went out to her. In most households this was a task delegated to children, but while she'd been gone, Mistress Patience had had to do everything alone.

Merrie silently walked to the intent woman and gently placed her hand over hers. "Let me take the handle," she said softly.

"Merrie!" Mistress Patience jumped up, startled. "I-I'm glad to see you!" Awkwardly, she patted Merrie's shoulder, and Merrie couldn't help but compare her show of love to Singing Wren's open-armed embrace. But Mistress Patience's eyes were suspiciously bright, as if from unshed tears, and she smiled warmly at Merrie. "I'm glad Zack gave me this duck. You are so thin! We'll have a good supper tonight!"

"How is Zack?" Merrie asked, her pulse quickening.

"Worried, too," Mistress Patience answered with a smile. "Every day he has gone into the woods searching for you."

"He has?" Merrie asked, astonished yet pleased.

"Where were you this past week?" Mistress Patience asked. "Are you all right?"

"It's a long story," Merrie said, smiling. "While I give the duck a turn, you sit and listen."

Mistress Patience readily agreed, settling herself in the rocker. With an absorbed look on her sweet but plain face, she watched Merrie, who briefly told her of the beaver trap ordeal and her stay with the Wampanoags.

When she'd finished, Mistress Patience,

lines on her forehead, stood and sympathetically touched Merrie's cheek. "You've been through a lot. I'm glad you found your way back safely. And," she added, an amused glint in her gray eyes, "I like your braids."

"I'm sure the Elders prefer it this way, too," Merrie replied archly.

"Yes, and Zack will also be pleased."

A slight frown darkened Merrie's face. She wondered if Zack really cared how she wore her hair, but she dismissed the thought. Right now she longed to see him. She looked at Patience, and, hiding her feelings, asked, "How have things been here?"

"Everyone has calmly accepted your punishment, but they've been worried, too."

"No one looked particularly worried when I walked into Plymouth," Merrie said bitterly. She wondered if Mistress Patience was one who took her punishment calmly. Or Zack.

"Luke Bosworth has been by every day, too. He brought me firewood." She indicated the split logs by the fireplace. "You know, he sails in two days."

Merrie was stunned. She had taken it for granted that the *Mayflower* would be anchored off Plymouth forever.

Mistress Patience motioned Merrie aside while she removed the browned duck from the iron spit and placed it on a wooden trencher.

"Has Master Loomis mentioned me?" Merrie asked casually, trying not to show her inner turmoil. "I wonder if he still hates me."

Mistress Patience sighed, wiping her hands

on her apron. "Ever since you left, Merrie, Master Loomis has been wearing a smug expression. I'm sure he never expected to see you again. He's an unforgiving man, and you'll give him a nasty jolt," she said. She shook her head.

"I think I can survive Master Loomis if I have the support of others," Merrie said, glancing at Mistress Patience from beneath her thick lashes.

Before supper, several Elders stopped by and informed Merrie she had fulfilled her punishment and was once again welcome in Plymouth. They warned her, however, that more misbehavior would result in permanent expulsion.

Merrie accepted their speeches graciously. She had no intention of ever again overstepping their bounds of good behavior.

After the Elders had gone, Merrie couldn't wait another minute. She had to see Zack. "Mistress Patience," she said, "I need to see Zack and tell him I'm all right. May I please find him? I'll be back soon." Her brown eyes pleaded for understanding.

"Run along," Mistress Patience said. "You may tell him he's invited for roast duck."

Merrie headed for the cornfield, her spirits soaring. She was glad to be home. Even if Little Fawn was her sister, this was where she belonged — where Zack was.

Half running, half skipping, she hummed a lilting tune as she hurried to where the men were working.

Arriving at the bottom of the field, she could see in the distance that the men, hoes on shoulders, had quit for the day.

As she ran, she heard her name called. Swinging about, she saw Luke.

"Wait, Merrie!" Luke broke into a run. His red hair was like a beacon, and he held his cap high in the air, waving it wildly.

Although it was good to see Luke's shining face, she wished he'd chosen a better time. Zack was the one she wanted to see now.

"Thank goodness you're back, Merrie!" he said, exuberantly scooping her into his powerful arms. "I was afraid I'd never see you again. I've thought about you every day. We sail in two days, Merrie. Will you come back with me?"

"I-I can't. . . ."

He smiled rakishly, touching a wisp of her hair. "Don't answer me now. I'll come by this evening. We've got a lot to talk about. Right now I need to get back to the ship and load provisions, or Captain Jones will have my hide. But I had to see you, Merrie. I thought I'd lost you." He laughed. "But here you are, more beautiful than ever, Merrie, my love!" He lifted her high in the air and whirled her about.

When he set her down, she was breathless, and his buoyant spirits made her laugh, too. "Luke! It's good to see you, too!"

Suddenly she glimpsed a tall dark figure in the background. Zack! Oh, Zack, she thought happily and, still smiling, she dashed to meet him, her hands outstretched. "Zack!" she cried happily. "I've thought about you every minute." She clasped his hands in hers. "You don't know how I've missed you."

A slight smile played across Zack's face. "It's good to see you, too, Merrie." But he released her hands quickly. "I see you've already been welcomed," he said coolly, but his dark eyes blazed when he glanced at Luke.

"I'm trying to convince Merrie she should sail back on the *Mayflower* with me," Luke said jovially.

"Really," Zack growled, his thick brows shooting upward.

Luke, arms folded, watched Zack, a slight twinkle in his blue eyes. "Don't you think that's a good idea, Zachariah?"

"That's up to Merrie, isn't it?" he asked evenly, but the chill in Zack's voice spread to her heart.

She stepped away from Zack, unable to believe what she'd heard. Surely Zack was joking — surely he didn't expect, for one instant, that she'd leave him and go with Luke!

"Zack," she choked. "Surely. . . ." She stopped.

Zack politely and coolly looked from her to Luke. "I didn't know you were thinking of going back to London, Merrie. Wasn't Jeremiah Farmingham the man you'd never marry?" he asked dryly. His mocking dark eyes swept over her.

"Who says she has to go back to old

Farmingham?" Luke protested, his compelling azure-blue eyes fastening on Merrie. "I'll protect her!"

"Luke!" she gasped, wondering what Zack must think.

"I see," Zack murmured, facing Merrie. "I didn't know you had a protector." A muscle rippled ominously along his square jaw. He wheeled about, his shoulders rigid, as he strode away.

"Zack," she shouted hoarsely, her heart pounding in her ears. Didn't he realize she loved him? "Zack! Don't go!"

But Zack didn't hear, or want to hear. Wretched, Merrie turned back to Luke, staring with dismay at his ruggedly handsome face.

Luke grabbed her hands. "Let him go, Merrie. A Pilgrim fellow doesn't deserve you. Not when you've got me." He grinned. "What more could you ask for?"

She felt a heavy sadness weighing her down. A tear slipped down her cheek.

"Ah, Merrie," Luke said, the animation suddenly leaving his face. "I'm sorry. I didn't mean to make you cry." Gently he wiped the teardrop away. "But can't you see, dear one, that you're not wanted here?"

Tears blinded her. Perhaps Luke was right.

Chapter Sixteen

MERRIE hadn't slept the night before, wondering whether to leave for England or stay. By dawn she'd made her decision. Even though she wanted to stay in Plymouth, she realized she'd never fit in. Obviously Zack thought she cared for Luke, and when she had tried to explain, he wouldn't listen. He'd simply walked away from her. Well, as Luke said, let him go. Tomorrow morning on the early tide, she'd sail on the *Mayflower*.

Later in the morning, she sadly packed a pair of black stockings and her wool dress, folding them and thrusting them into a woven basket. She piled in a pair of gloves, a Pilgrim cap, which she seldom wore, two petticoats, and some dried herbs. She hadn't arrived with much, and she wouldn't go back with much.

She felt her throat tighten but was determined not to cry. She had shed her tears yesterday. Now that she'd made her choice she was almost looking forward to home. She wanted to see Father again. And she'd like to sleep in her soft bed and wear her beautiful clothes. She'd throw away her red wool and the gingham dress she was wearing. Smoothing her skirt, she remembered how hard she'd worked on every stitch. No, she couldn't throw away this dress.

She thought about her father and was surprised by a stab of longing. Would he be glad to see her after an eight-month absence? Surely he'd relent about Jeremiah and let her decide whom she'd marry. Maybe she'd even meet someone more handsome, more tender, and more fun than Zack. Maybe, she thought, but highly unlikely.

She combed her hair, letting it tumble down her back. She'd wear it long and flowing just to spite Master Loomis. She almost hoped she'd meet him. Today was her last day in Plymouth, so let him glower and rave. She didn't care.

She wouldn't think of Zack any longer, either. She had to tell him good-bye, but she wasn't certain he wanted to see her. Would he miss her? she wondered. Defiantly, she tied a red sash around her waist, promising to forget Zack. She willed herself not to cry. No matter what she told herself, Zack was the one she loved.

She sighed. She needed to say her good-byes. Today she'd go to Sowans to see Little

Fawn. In the morning she'd say good-bye to Mistress Patience.

As Merrie hurried along the forest path, the sun filtered through the budding trees, feeling warm on her back. A bluebird trilled a sweet song from high above, and she smelled the sweet scent of wild strawberries tinged with the odor of ocean salt spray. She'd miss the woods, the animals, the river, and the ocean.

Coming near Sowans, she glimpsed a group of Indian women gathering the sweet sap of the maple trees into birchbark buckets. As Merrie came closer, she saw Little Fawn on her knees. She kneeled down beside her. "Can I help?" she smiled.

"Merrie!" Little Fawn exclaimed. "I am glad to see you. But you have come back so soon to Sowans!"

"Yes," Merrie answered, scooping boiled syrup from the trough and pouring it into molds to crystallize. "Something happened," she said evenly. "I'll be leaving Plymouth tomorrow."

"No," Little Fawn said in dismay, her oval face worried.

"Do you have to stay here and make maple sugar?" Merrie asked.

Singing Wren was nearby. "You go with Merrie, Little Fawn."

Little Fawn rose with a grateful gesture toward her mother and walked with Merrie along the sandy shore of the fishing stream.

Merrie felt good just being near Little Fawn. She could talk to her. She was her own age and would understand her problem.

Little Fawn pointed to a weeping willow. "Let us sit there."

"Yes," Merrie agreed. "I have a lot to tell you." As they strolled arm in arm they passed two Indian warriors balancing a pair of heavy logs about three feet off the ground on several spindly posts with a large rock on top.

"What are they making?" Merrie asked.

Little Fawn's eyes warmed as she raised her hand to a young warrior. He stopped and smiled. He was tall, and as lean and lithe as Little Fawn herself. Finally, Little Fawn said, "They are making a trap to catch a bear."

The warrior who had smiled at Little Fawn attached a chunk of deer meat to one of the posts.

"When the bear comes," Little Fawn explained, "it grabs the meat. The poles collapse and rock and logs fall and kill it. It's a deadfall trap."

"I see," Merrie said, but she wasn't really interested in how a deadfall trap worked. "Who was the brave who smiled at you?" she asked.

"Silver Fox," Little Fawn said in a low voice, a slight smile hovering about her lips.

They reached the willow and settled down under the trailing branches.

"Little Fawn," Merrie prodded, "who is Silver Fox? You haven't told me about him."

"Silver Fox calls on me. We will marry soon."

"Do you love him?" Merrie asked.

"Yes," Little Fawn said shyly, plucking a blade of grass and twirling it in her slender fingers.

"And does he love you?"

Little Fawn nodded, touching the foxtail attached to her belt. "He gave me his symbol."

"You're lucky," Merrie said simply, feeling a twinge of envy. "I'm in love, too, but Zack doesn't love me like I love him."

"I'm sorry you're going back," Little Fawn said, taking Merrie's hand and rubbing it against her smooth cheek. "I will miss my sister."

Merrie looked at Little Fawn. "You have an honored place in your tribe, Little Fawn. In Plymouth, I'm an outsider and have no one to love. You have Silver Fox."

"Yes, it is important to be loved. But you are loved at Sowans, Merrie. Stay here."

"No, Little Fawn, thank you, but it is time to go back to my own people."

Little Fawn frowned. "Aren't Pilgrims your own people, Merrie?"

Merrie paused. "Well, yes, in a way," she replied, "but it is sort of like the Wampanoags and Narraganset. You war with Narraganset. The two tribes have different customs."

"But Pilgrims are all English white people, yes?" Little Fawn persisted.

Merrie chuckled. "Come," she said, leaping up. "I don't want to think of London. I want to enjoy the woods today and just be with you. Let's make flower garlands." The two girls raced into the forest clearing and, laughing and chattering, they picked jonquils and daisies.

The day at Sowans had passed quickly. All too soon Merrie had to say her good-byes to Singing Wren, Black Eagle, and Chief Massasoit, and as she followed a deer trail and wended her way back to Plymouth, a throbbing ache started in her throat when she realized she'd never see them again.

Coming into the colony, she passed the town well, where several women had gathered. Mary Brewster came to tell her good-bye and wish her a happy voyage, but Merrie noticed she didn't urge her to remain.

Merrie glanced around at the rude houses and garden plots. She had helped build this settlement, she thought achingly, and inside felt a strong pull to stay. She paused before her cabin, admiring the small garden she and Mistress Patience had planted. She took a deep breath when she realized she'd never see the green corn shoots or the squash grow. The green glossy leaves of the tulips were sprouting, however. Soon the bright blossoms would unfold.

Mistress Patience came out with a long-strawed broom. "The front stoop needs sweeping," she said lamely.

Merrie looked at her steadily, wanting to run and hug her, but she wasn't certain of

Mistress Patience's feelings. Perhaps she was glad she was leaving — not that Mistress Patience didn't love her, but perhaps Merrie Courtland had become an embarrassment to her.

"Zack came by with a rabbit," Mistress Patience said, "but I think it was an excuse to see you."

"Did you tell him I'm leaving?" Merrie asked, holding her breath.

"Yes, I told him. I know he wants you to stay." She glanced down at Merrie, who sat on the stoop, and said quietly with a wan smile, "So do I."

Merrie felt a surge of hope. Did Zack want her to stay? And Mistress Patience, too? "Did Zack really say he wanted me to stay?" she questioned.

"Well," Mistress Patience hesitated, leaning on her broom, "not in so many words, but I could tell. . . ."

"He didn't ask me to stay, did he?" Merrie said, her buoyant hope suddenly dashed.

"No," Mistress Patience said, then paused. "But here he comes now. Why don't you ask him yourself?"

Merrie glanced up, and, sure enough, Zack was striding down the lane. She was certain her pounding heart could be heard above the ocean's roar.

"I'll skin the rabbit for your last dinner at home," Mistress Patience said, discreetly going inside.

Zack stopped in front of Merrie and

propped one foot up on the stoop. "I hear you're leaving tomorrow."

"Yes," Merrie said softly, meeting his eyes and willing him to beg her to stay.

"I hope you and Luke will be happy," he said, his voice level but with his dark eyes studying her intently.

She had to make him understand, she thought. "I-I want to stay here, Zack, but ..."

"But Luke wants you to go back with him, is that it?" Zack asked, his lips pressed in a thin smile.

"No," she whispered, "it isn't like that...."

"Zachariah!" Oliver Loomis called in a harsh voice, hurrying forward. He glared at Merrie but didn't acknowledge her. "I need to see you about the traps you've set along Beaver Trail."

Zack nodded, his eyes never leaving Merrie's face. "Are you certain you're doing the right thing, Merrie?"

"I-I don't know," she said, the words barely escaping past her tight throat. She wished he'd forbid her to go, to say that her place was here in Plymouth. With him!

"News travels fast, Mistress Courtland," Oliver Loomis said smoothly, finally speaking to her. "I understand you're sailing tomorrow." He swept off his high crowned hat, and his wispy thin hair blew around his narrow face. "I hope you have a good trip."

And, good riddance, you should add, she thought bitterly. This man who had caused her so much grief could afford to be gracious

— now that she was leaving. "Thank you, Master Loomis," she said evenly, rising to her feet. Her cheeks burned when she met his cold eyes. How he must be laughing inside! But she wouldn't show her defeat. He'd only gloat all the more. She tossed back her long hair in a gesture of defiance and abruptly turned her back on him to face Zack. For an instant her eyes met his, and she drank in his strong, lean features. "Then . . ." she choked, "this is good-bye?"

"This is good-bye," Zack said slowly. "What time do you leave?"

"Luke is rowing me out to the *Mayflower* at dawn."

Zack stood, watching her. "Luke," he murmured, with a slight knowing nod and a bitter smile.

Why didn't Zack leave? Her anxious thoughts made her stomach knot and churn. Was there still a chance? Hesitantly, she lifted her hand, holding it out to him.

Zack's eyes warmed, and he took a step forward.

Master Loomis impatiently pulled on Zack's sleeve. "I need to show you the traps before dark," he snapped.

Zack, with a sadness in his eyes she'd never seen before, said gently, "I'll never forget you."

"And I'll always remember you," she said, a catch in her voice.

"Zachariah!" Master Loomis shouted. "Are you coming or aren't you?"

With a last glance at Merrie, Zack wheeled about and strode away, accompanying Master Loomis toward the river.

She stared after him until his tall, rangy figure was out of sight. She'd never find anyone else like Zack. Never. She bit her lip to keep back her tears of despair. Sorrowfully, she turned and went indoors to finish packing.

Chapter Seventeen

AFTER Merrie had eaten supper, she set her meager belongings by the door, ready for her morning departure.

She glanced at Mistress Patience, who busily scoured a pewter platter with sand. Dismally, she undressed and slipped into her nightgown, throwing back the feather coverlet on her bunk.

Patience, putting down the platter, said in her gentle manner, "Merrie, come and sit by the fire with me."

Merrie mustered a bleak smile. She didn't want to make Mistress Patience miserable, too.

She sat before the crackling logs, hugging her knees to her, while Mistress Patience leaned back in the rocker. For a while they were silent, watching the sparks shoot up the chimney.

At last Mistress Patience spoke, dropping

her hand on Merrie's shoulder, "I want to give you a gift to remember me by."

Startled, Merrie glanced back into Mistress Patience's shining dove-gray eyes. Was it the firelight or love that glowed with such warmth, Merrie wondered. "You-you don't have to give me anything," she protested, not knowing how to react to this show of affection.

"I know I don't, Merrie," the quiet woman said, and reached into her pocket, pulling forth a brooch, "but I want to." The silver oval pin, carved with an intricate floral design, had two silver petals dangling from the bottom rim. She pressed it into Merrie's hand.

Merrie gasped at the pin's exquisite beauty. Speechless, she traced the filigree design with her forefinger. Not at all what a Pilgrim woman would wear, she thought. Where would Mistress Patience get such a brooch?

As if in answer to her thoughts, Mistress Patience said, "It was my mother's."

"Your mother's?" Merrie echoed lamely. "I-I can't accept such a present. You must keep it."

Mistress Patience closed Merrie's fingers over it. "No, I want you to have it. Please."

Merrie nodded. "If that's what you want," she murmured. "I'd love to have a remembrance of you." She clutched the pin to her breast and glanced at Mistress Patience. "Where did your mother get it?"

"Before Queen Elizabeth died in 1603, Mother was an attendant at her court."

Mistress Patience smiled wistfully, and her hair looked more silver than brown in the blazing firelight. "Her name was Lady Anne, and she was lovely. Her husband, Sir Peter Winston, was one of Elizabeth's 'Sea Dogs' and went down with his ship in the fight with the Spanish Armada in 1588. I was just a baby. Heartbroken, Mother continued to dance and play the lute for Elizabeth." She sighed lightly. "When I married Daniel, she was already very ill — she died a short time later, leaving me her jewels. Daniel and I agreed they should be used for the Separatist cause."

"You gave all your mother's jewels to the Pilgrims?" Merrie asked.

"Yes, all but this one," Mistress Patience said, taking the brooch from Merrie. "I cherished this piece all these years. Now," she said, pinning it to Merrie's nightgown, "I want it to be worn by someone I love." Her eyes glistened, and Merrie's heavy heart lightened.

Suddenly, she turned and clasped Mistress Patience's legs and buried her face in her lap. "Oh, Mistress Patience, I love you, too. I do, I do," she cried. "But I thought you wanted me to leave — that I'd shamed you. Even if I served my punishment, some still shun me. Why should you risk humiliation because of me?"

"Is that what you think?" Mistress Patience said, stroking Merrie's hair. "I've grown to love you, Merrie." She chuckled softly. "If you're too free-spirited at times, I can understand. I wish you didn't have to leave."

Merrie lifted her tear-stained face. "I have to. Zack doesn't want me . . . and . . ." She let her voice fade as she once again rested her head against Mistress Patience's knee.

"Are you committed to sailing tomorrow?" Mistress Patience asked, lifting Merrie's face between her two hands.

"Yes, I-I must," Merrie said in a low, tormented tone.

"If you change your mind, you have a home here. I'll always love you. You're like my daughter."

Merrie said nothing. She couldn't.

The two women sat together until long after the night owl's calling, sharing an evening of silent loving companionship.

When Merrie went to bed, she was filled with a peaceful contentment. At last she felt fully accepted by Mistress Patience. And she understood Mistress Patience better, too. If Patience was quietly unassuming and hid her emotions, that was her way.

But her contentment was disrupted by images of Zack. When she thought of his rejection of her, her emotions spiraled downward. Could one be happy and sad at the same time? She wondered if Zack was sleeping. Or was he lying awake as she was? Did her leaving trouble him? When she thought of their anguished meeting yesterday, with Oliver Loomis glowering and pulling Zack away from her, she wanted to leap out of bed and see Zack one last time. He hadn't even kissed her good-bye. When they'd parted, she thought he'd made a move to stop her, but maybe that was her imagination.

Furiously, she twisted and turned. Would sleep never come?

Well, she grimly told herself, if Zack didn't want her, Luke did. The lighthearted sailor loved her and was good to her. After all, she thought, a sea captain's wife would lead a thrilling life, one of excitement. And she had no doubt Luke would become a captain some-day — he was bright, ambitious, and knew the sea. He was a natural leader. She'd seen how the crew listened to him.

He had a way with men. She tossed on her side, a brief smile touching her lips. Luke had a way with women, too. Yes, there could be worse things than returning to Courtland Manor. And they'd return much faster. Per-haps the voyage would take only a month, Luke had said, because there wouldn't be the winter storms to hinder them.

Of course, Father would welcome her with open arms — if he wasn't too preoccupied with wool shipments. Then he'd decide her future. It would be difficult to become his dutiful daughter again, she mused. She had become too independent in Plymouth. Inde-pendent was different from being headstrong. Stowing away on the *Mayflower* had been headstrong.

Would she do it again? Yes, oh, yes, she

thought. If she hadn't stowed away she'd never have met Zack, never have found a mother. Now she had two — Mistress Patience and Singing Wren. She stared into the darkness. What would Father think of Luke? Would he let her choose a sailor over a wealthy merchant? Perhaps if he thought that sailor had the stuff of a captain.

And she'd see Nancy Bates, her best friend. No, she thought, Little Fawn had replaced Nancy. At any rate, Nancy would want to hear all about her adventures in Plymouth. Then when she'd told half her story, Nancy would interrupt to tell her about the latest plays and the teas she'd been invited to . . . and, oh, Merrie thought gloomily, tossing on the bed, she didn't want to go back to that life! She wasn't the same person as she'd been then. Deliberately she closed her eyes, but still sleep eluded her. Her jumbled thoughts were like fireflies darting in and out of her mind: Mistress Patience, Zack, Father, Jeremiah Farmingham, Luke, Little Fawn, Nancy Bates, Oliver Loomis.

After a long and difficult night, Merrie finally dozed. When she opened her eyes to the first glimmerings of dawn peeping through the edges of the greased paper over the window, she quietly rose and dressed. Luke would be at the beach waiting for her. She glanced at Mistress Patience, who stirred in bed. Without lingering under the covers, Patience got up and dressed.

Merrie opened the door, looking down the

path where Miles Standish lived. Was Zack up? In the gray morning light she glimpsed a figure beside the front door. Her heart beat faster, but the spark of hope was soon extinguished. It was Miles Standish himself in full armor, ready to drill his troops. He inspected his men and their muskets daily and had them march in formation. He insisted on being prepared in case the Indians became hostile. She peered closer. Was Zack still sleeping? Surely not. He knew she was leaving at dawn.

Listlessly, she went back inside and ate the johnnycake that Mistress Patience had prepared. The thin corn cake tasted flat and heavy, but she was reluctant to finish it. The time had come to leave.

Getting up from the table, she threw her cloak around her shoulders and looked into the mirror to tie her brown wool scarf around her bright heavy hair. A few golden strands escaped, framing her face. Merrie was amazed at her reflection. Beneath her rosy color her face was pinched and drawn. From her liquid brown eyes shone something besides raw hurt.

It was an inner strength she hadn't known before. Even her slender figure seemed to show the physical strength she'd developed. Her lean cheeks, straight short nose, firm chin, and soft curves indicated she was a woman now. You must act grown-up, she sternly told herself. Inside, though, she wanted to cry.

She turned, picked up her basket, and ran

to kiss Mistress Patience good-bye. For a moment, Merrie clung to her, then abruptly spun about and dashed out the door toward the sea.

Luke was already there. When he caught sight of her, he jumped out of the rowboat and splashed ashore, wetting his high boots to the knees.

"M'lady," he said with a mock bow and, sweeping off his knit cap, "your carriage awaits." He helped her into the small boat and picked up the oars.

Merrie gazed at Plymouth. No one had come to see her off. It was just as well. Wasn't it?

Captain Jones helped Merrie aboard the *Mayflower*. She walked up the gangplank slowly. "There's a fine little cabin for you behind the forecastle, Merrie," Captain Jones told her.

"Thank you," she murmured, thinking how pleasant he was compared with when he'd discovered her as a stowaway last summer.

"This way," Luke said, picking up her basket. Walking along the deck, he whispered in her ear, "I'm glad you're coming back with me. You'll make the voyage perfect!"

She stopped at the rail, looking down at the swirling waters. Terrible doubts and regrets washed over her as she realized it was too late to go back. The sails were being hoisted.

Chapter
Eighteen

TREMBLING, Merrie watched the water lapping against the ship's hull. She had a nauseating, sinking feeling of despair. Why am I leaving? she asked herself with frantic helplessness. Was it too late to undo her action?

Suddenly, she whirled about, her cloak and hair flying, and faced Luke. "I've got to go back!" she shouted, her eyes wild with urgency. "I can't sail for England."

Luke stared at her as if she'd lost her mind. "What are you saying, Merrie? The anchor's ready to be hauled up." He grabbed her arms and faced her. His clear blue eyes bored into hers. "I want you to go with me. Whatever you have to face in London, I'll be at your side. Don't be afraid!"

"I'm not afraid, Luke," she answered as calmly as possible.

"Then, what is it?" he asked, letting go of her and standing back. His hands rested on his hips, and his sturdy legs were planted far apart. When she didn't answer, he repeated harshly, "If you're not afraid, why don't you want to go back?"

She felt the panic rise in her throat as orders were barked and one sailor scurried up the rigging. Others raced past her. She had to hurry before they sailed. Glancing at the dark water, she thought of jumping and swimming to shore. Then she shuddered, remembering how Dorothy Bradford had drowned.

"Look, Merrie," Luke said, his tone and eyes softening. "I love you. I'm asking you to come back with me."

She shook her head, and gently placed her hand on his arm. "I love Zack, Luke. I must go to him. If I return to England, I'll never be happy. Never. I belong in Plymouth. I'm a colonist," she said proudly.

"And who says you are?" he growled, his red hair gleaming crimson-gold in the morning sun. "If you ask me, I haven't seen the Pilgrims treat you right! Most of them will be glad you're gone!"

"Please," she begged. "Take me back, Luke."

"I haven't seen Zack exactly rush to stop you from leaving," he argued.

"You're right," she said, gazing at him steadily, "and I don't know if he wants to see me now. But I must find out." She flung out her hands, hopelessly. "Help me, Luke." Her voice cracked. "We've got to hurry!"

Luke touched her cheek wistfully. "Then, if that's what you want, I'll take you back," he said gruffly. He tipped his head toward the rowboat. "Let's go." He gave her a half smile. "But I think you're making a mistake."

"One of many I've made in Plymouth," she said dryly, moving rapidly toward the rope ladder. She felt as if a stone had been lifted from her heart.

Luke spoke to Captain Jones, who looked in Merrie's direction and saluted her with his long-stemmed pipe. Then, dismissing her for more pressing problems, he turned to his first mate.

Climbing down the ladder, Merrie's heart thundered in her ears. Hadn't she told herself to act grown-up? And now, after making an agonizing decision, she'd changed her mind in one split second. What will Mistress Patience think of me?

When they reached the shore, Luke jumped clear of the boat, offered Merrie his hand, and faced her. "I'll never forget you, Merrie Courtland," he said, smiling.

The rushing waves rolled up onto the sandy beach, swirling about their feet, but Merrie didn't notice. "Luke," she said warmly, "you've been wonderful. I've been a silly girl, not knowing my own mind."

"Zack is a lucky fellow," he growled, squarely meeting her eyes. Overhead a gull circled and cawed. All at once he pulled her into his arms and kissed her.

Merrie stepped back. Softly, she touched his cheek with the palm of her hand.

Luke took a deep breath, then grinned. "That was so you wouldn't forget me, Merrie." But although his tone was light and mocking, there was a hurt in his eyes she wished she could make go away.

He touched two fingers to his cap and swiftly walked to the boat.

She watched as he rowed to the *Mayflower*. He cupped his hands around his mouth and shouted over the pounding surf, "I love you, Merrie. I'll sign on the crew for the next ship bound for Plymouth."

Dear Luke, she thought, and smiled, wiping away a tear. "Good-bye, Luke," she called, but her words were lost on the rising wind.

Returning to Mistress Patience's cabin, Merrie went inside and dropped her belongings. Mistress Patience looked up from her spinning wheel in astonishment. She jumped up and joyfully hugged Merrie as if she'd never let her go. Finally, she released her and stepped back, looking warmly into Merrie's eyes. "Go and find him. I saw him heading for the river a short while ago," she said with a knowing smile.

So Zack hadn't even stood on the shore to watch the ship sail, she thought sorrowfully.

Following the Deer Trail, Merrie rehearsed what she'd say, but as she neared the river, her steps slowed and her heart thudded painfully. What can I say to Zack? she thought. What if he won't talk to me? She clenched her fists. She'd make him listen. But had she done the right thing? At least Luke loved her and offered her a whole different life, a life that was fast vanishing with the departure of the *Mayflower*!

She pushed away the wild strawberry branches and stepped along the marshy part of the river where cattails grew, thick and tall.

Unexpectedly, she glimpsed Zack, sitting with his back against a white birch and listlessly tossing one pebble after another into the water. His long booted legs were stretched before him, and his black hair ruffled in the breeze. For a moment she stood mesmerized, studying his dark, brooding face. What was he thinking, she wondered.

Abruptly, on the clear still air, drifted the faint cry from the *Mayflower*: "Lift anchor!"

With a groan, Zack leaped to his feet. "Merrie!" he called, desperately running his fingers through his black hair. "Merrie, how could I let you go?" For an instant his body was rigid and his face anguished, then suddenly he began to run toward the ocean.

His words sent her heart soaring, and she hurriedly stepped out from the willows, directly in his path.

Startled, Zack stopped in his tracks. "Merrie," he whispered, unbelievingly. "What. . . ?"

"What am I doing here?" She finished his

sentence with a smile. Suddenly she blushed and couldn't meet his eyes. What must he think of her boldness? Shyly, she said, "I couldn't leave you, Zack."

All at once she felt Zack's strong arms about her, and his lips pressing on hers. Happiness flowed inside like a sun-splashed river, and she wrapped her arms about him, her fingers intertwined in his thick hair. All of her previous doubts were gone.

"Merrie," he said huskily against her hair. "I thought I'd lost you!"

She nestled closer in his arms, unable to reply.

Zack's black eyes, sparkling with love, studied every line of her face. "Don't ever leave me again, Merrie."

"Never, never," she replied softly. She was with the man she loved. And to think she'd almost given him up and run away.

"I love you, Merrie," Zack said simply, and tilted up her chin with his thumb so he could kiss her again.

His lips were soft and sweet on hers.

"Tell me," Zack said, grinning down at her, "do you love me?"

"Do I have to tell you?" she said, smiling impishly despite the swell of gladness in her throat. "Isn't my being here proof enough?"

Zack gave a low, rich laugh. "I guess it is," he said, sitting down on the bank and pulling her beside him.

They sat and talked until Zack had to leave for the fields.

Walking along the path, Merrie said, "Master Loomis will be furious when he discovers I've come back." She cast a worried look at Zack.

"Don't worry about gloomy Oliver," he said. "Do you know that yesterday when he wanted me to look at the traps I couldn't find anything wrong?" He shook his head.

Of course not, Merrie thought. He only wanted to get you away from me. But she said nothing. She only hoped Master Loomis wouldn't create more trouble.

"Master Loomis can't separate us, Merrie," Zack said confidently, and his white teeth flashed against his dark skin. "He might even learn to like you."

"I never did believe in fairy tales," she replied. "But I don't care if he hates me. As long as I have you, I can face anything."

She and Zack strolled into Plymouth, her arm casually linked through his. She had a spring to her step, and she nodded pleasantly at people working in their gardens.

Look at us, she wanted to shout gleefully. I'm in love with Zack, and he's in love with me. Could there be a happier day?

Suddenly, coming toward them was the all-too-familiar gaunt figure of Oliver Loomis, his great black cloak flapping about his stilt-like legs.

"Zachariah!" he said stiffly. "I need to talk to you!"

At his words, Merrie's blood ran cold. Was he again trying to ruin their relationship?

"What is it, Oliver?" Zack asked, not removing his arm from Merrie's, the smile never leaving his face.

"It's Governor Carver!" Master Loomis said with a sense of immediacy in his harsh voice. "He's gravely ill. They've just carried him in from the fields."

Zack frowned. "Where is he?" he asked shortly.

"In his cabin," Master Loomis said, giving Merrie a withering look. "This is a dark day for everyone."

Zack squeezed Merrie's hand. "I'll be back soon." He broke into a run, racing toward John Carver's house.

Merrie was left alone, facing Master Loomis.

"Well," Master Loomis said. "I see you've come crawling back to Plymouth. I thought we'd rid ourselves of vermin like you!" He poked his thin face into hers and sneered, "And now with your wiles you've even hypnotized one of our most upstanding young men! Well, Zachariah Gaines will find you out just as I did!" Glaring down at her, he flung his cloak around himself and stood like a great black pillar. "You won't last long this time, either." He laughed harshly. "One misstep and the Pilgrims will chase you back to England, where you belong."

Merrie had had enough of his insinuations and insults! Straightening her shoulders and holding her head high, she boldly met his icy stare. "Why are you so desperate to see me leave Plymouth, Master Loomis?" She folded her arms across her chest. "You've been hounding me ever since I arrived!"

"Ever since you stowed away, you mean! You're nothing but a little sneak, and I intend to see you pay for what you did!"

His accusing tone sent a prickle of fear up her back, and the warm breeze that had felt so delightful on her skin a short time ago now warmed her uncomfortably.

"I have people to side with me — to help me," she retorted sharply.

"And who would help you?" he snarled, a look of surprise on his thin face.

"Zack, for one," she said. "And Mistress Patience!"

"Widow Patience, you mean." He snickered disdainfully. "As if a lone widow woman could help you!"

"And," she said, plunging recklessly on, "I have friends in Sowans. Even a blood sister, Little Fawn!"

"A blood sister!" Oliver Loomis's eyebrows shot up, and he observed her through hooded, glittering eyes. "So you've wormed your way in with the Indians. I'm not surprised. You're just like them! Indians can't be trusted, either, and they'd like to slit our throats while we sleep."

"That's not true!" Merrie shouted, feeling hot blood rush to her face. "The Wampanoags are our friends! Without them we'd never have survived the winter!"

A brittle smile flickered across his face but

never reached his cold, distant eyes. "It's just as I suspected! Your loyalty is with the Indians, Mistress Courtland. I thought as much. You think you've made friends here, but I'd be careful if I were you," he warned softly. "Very careful! You're a girl who schemes and plots to further her own interests! Soon others will catch on to your intrigues, too."

"I don't scheme or plot, Master Loomis," she said evenly. "It's your imagination!"

"My imagination?" He snorted. "That's what you'd like me to believe. We'll see, Mistress Courtland, if it's only my imagination when you find yourself on the next ship out of here!" With his cloak swirling about him, he stalked away, muttering, "Little Fawn, indeed!"

Chapter Nineteen

For the next six weeks Merrie avoided Master Loomis, and the days she didn't see him were happy and contented ones. She worked alongside Mistress Patience and frequently saw Zack. Life, since the death of fifty-four-year-old John Carver, had settled into a pleasant routine. William Bradford had been elected the new governor and had chosen as his assistant Isaac Allerton. The first wedding, between Susanna White, widowed during the winter, and Edward Winslow, the newly appointed Indian ambassador, had taken place.

For the first time since the Pilgrims had arrived, food was plentiful, although getting used to a different diet was difficult for some. Merrie couldn't understand them. It seemed they'd rather starve than eat the fresh fish

over the salted. Nor did they like such delicacies as eel, oyster, clams, lobster, cod, and
bass, which Merrie found a real treat. But
their staple diet of dried peas, beans, oatmeal,
salt beef, salt pork, bread, and cheese now
began to include New England food: deer,
partridge, duck, turkey, goose, and all kinds
of berries.

On a Sunday morning in July, Merrie
dressed in her dark gingham dress, and although her abundant hair was done up in a
bun, she couldn't keep a few wisps from flying
free. Sundays, for Saints and Strangers alike,
were always the same, she thought wearily.
Everyone went to church, with no exceptions.
At least, even though William Brewster's
sermons were two hours long, he was a good
speaker and often a stirring one.

Zack, fully armed with sword and musket,
now escorted them to the fort, where services
were held, and, like everyone, she, Mistress
Patience, and Zack walked in threes. From
Saturday afternoons until Sunday sunset no
work was allowed. No housework, not even
cooking a hot meal, and certainly not any
farming. Besides that, you couldn't fish, shoot,
sail, row, or jump.

The warm spring day with the scent of wild
roses in the air was pleasant, and today
Merrie planned to enjoy sitting in the
Common House. She would let her mind
wander and think of Zack and what the
future might bring. In her heart she sang

the madrigal that was sung at Susanna
White's wedding:

> My bonnie lass she smileth
> And she my heart beguileth
> Smile less, dear love, therefore,
> And you shall love me more.

The warm sun meant she'd no longer freeze
during the church service or have to carry her
foot warmer. This past winter the wind had
whistled beneath the oiled paper at the windows and through the chinks between the
logs.

Entering the fort, Zack went to the men's
section of the Common House, and she and
Mistress Patience sat on the hard wooden
bench next to Mary Brewster. Once the
sermon started, Merrie watched the brass-
trimmed hourglass, wondering if the watch-
man or tithingman would turn it once or
twice today.

The tithingman stood beside the young
boys who sat together and who most frequently needed his attention. She smiled when
she saw Johnny Billington punch Matthew
Brewster. The tithingman's long stick, with
the hard wooden knob on one end, came down
hard on Johnny's skull. As Merrie gazed
straight ahead at the tall pulpit, she thought
of tomorrow, when she'd meet Little Fawn at
Willow Cove. Squanto had given Little Fawn
her message, and she wondered what Little

Fawn had thought when she'd heard Merrie hadn't sailed after all.

Merrie glanced toward the men's section and felt her cheeks pinken when she met Zack's eyes. Modestly, she looked down at her folded hands. Closing her eyes, for a moment she relived Zack's first tender kiss.

Suddenly, something tickled her nose. She brushed at it. Then to her embarrassment she looked up to see the tithingman. The end of his pole, with a foxtail attached, was under her nose. She knew its purpose — to awaken anyone dozing off. Blushing furiously, she tried not to notice Mistress Patience's disapproving glance or Master Loomis's smug little smile. Instead, she focused on Elder Brewster standing in the high pulpit, impressively dressed in his violet suit. But the nagging thought of Oliver Loomis observing her attention lapse in church unsettled her.

The next day Merrie had forgotten about the meetinghouse incident, and, as she traveled through the woods, she wondered if Little Fawn had missed her as much as she'd missed her blood sister. Patience had promised she could stay overnight at Sowans, and her heart felt as light and sweet as the yellow canary's song overhead.

Merrie watched her footing as she stepped lightly along a rocky slope above the river's sparkling blue waters. From a small crack in the rock, water trickled from the face of the shale to splash into the river below.

At last Merrie reached the sandy riverbank. From a distance she glimpsed Little Fawn, who was sitting beneath a weeping willow and combing her long, shining hair.

"Little Fawn!" Merrie called.

Little Fawn looked up alertly. When she saw Merrie, she sprang to her feet and ran to meet her.

The two girls flung their arms about each other.

"I thought I lost you," Little Fawn said. "You did not sail on the *Mayflower*?"

"I changed my mind," Merrie said, her dark eyes smiling.

"Was it Zack?" Little Fawn asked knowingly.

Merrie nodded. Little Fawn understood her feelings.

"Now you have a man, too," Little Fawn said. "Soon, you will marry Zack like I will marry Silver Fox."

Merrie laughed, and the tinkling sound echoed over the rippling river. "I don't know, Little Fawn. That remains to be seen."

Little Fawn hugged her again. "I'm glad you are back. Singing Wren will prepare special food for you."

"I can't wait to see her and Black Eagle."

"We need to go to Sowans. I am glad you can stay tonight. We have so much to talk about."

Arriving in the Indian village, Merrie ran to greet Singing Wren, who embraced her. Little Fawn's mother had prepared roast venison for the occasion. Black Eagle, too, was glad to see her and asked about Plymouth and its crops.

Long after everyone was in bed, Little Fawn and Merrie sat before the campfire and talked. Merrie told her that Oliver Loomis was determined to force her from Plymouth, and how he constantly watched her. Little Fawn sympathized. Then, poking at the fire, she said, "We have problem in Sowans, too."

Merrie was concerned, realizing she'd only been thinking about herself. "What is it, Little Fawn? Can I help?"

"No," Little Fawn said. "Corbitant, a sachem loyal to Chief Massasoit, now urges war against his chief. Chief Massasoit is afraid Corbitant will side with his enemy, the Narragansets."

"But that's terrible, Little Fawn," Merrie said. "If the Narragansets ever found out that Governor Bradford has only twenty-two armed men, they'd attack Plymouth right away."

"Sachem Corbitant hates Plymouth," Little Fawn said. "He hates Squanto most of all because he helped the white people. Corbitant wants all white people killed. He wants Squanto killed, too."

"I must warn Governor Bradford," Merrie said, suddenly frightened. She thought of how the settlers had survived a harsh winter and sealed their peace with Chief Massasoit. Did they now have to fight hostile Indians?

"Chief Massasoit has gone to see the Narragansets on a peace mission," Little Fawn said, a shadow darkening her face. "He comes back in the morning. Then we know — peace or war." Her face brightened. "Black Eagle is teaching Chief Massasoit to talk the white language. He can make peace now in Indian and English."

Merrie stared into the flames, hoping with all her heart that the chief spoke a clear peace language with the Narragansets. She didn't care what language it was. Just so the Narragansets didn't declare war on Plymouth.

The next morning Merrie prepared to leave Sowans but wanted to wait and see Chief Massasoit. However, when the chief still hadn't arrived by noon, she said her good-byes.

As she hurried past the wigwams and out the palisades gate, an Indian runner, squat and fat, rushed by her.

Merrie spun about and followed him. If he had news of Chief Massasoit, she had to hear his message.

She joined the circle of Indians, listening to the breathless messenger. Although she didn't understand him, she could tell by his arrogant stance, haughty stare, and loud tone, that he was giving the Wampanoags bad news.

Little Fawn hastened to Merrie's side, quickly translating. "The messenger says Chief Massasoit will not be returning. He must stay with the Narragansets!"

With frightened eyes Merrie looked at Little Fawn. "What does that mean?"

"I think Chief Massasoit is a prisoner of the Narragansets," Little Fawn replied evenly.

Merrie gasped. "I must warn Governor Bradford," she said, breathing hard. Then she touched Little Fawn's wrist. "I must go!"

"Yes, go. Fast!" Little Fawn said urgently. "Go," Little Fawn urged. "Fast!"

Merrie turned and ran toward the gate.

The messenger twisted about, shouting at her.

Merrie didn't stop, even though the plump messenger began to chase her.

Chapter Twenty

Although Merrie knew the way back to Plymouth, she wasn't certain this advantage would help her. She was no match for an Indian runner. This messenger, however, was wheezing and overweight. Perhaps after all, she could outrun him.

She had to think of something fast. Her tracks blended with the dusty footprints around the palisades, but once into the forest he'd easily be able to follow her.

Without hesitating, Merrie ran in the direction of the river. If she ran in the water, she'd have a good chance of outwitting him. He couldn't track her there. She knew how to swim, too. She hoped she could lose him before she reached the river, but if he got too close, she'd hold her breath underwater.

As her thoughts raced with her feet, she thanked Little Fawn over and over for the silent moccasins. Why did this messenger want to prevent her from reaching Plymouth? Were the Narragansets afraid of the Pilgrims? Did they want to stop a rescue attempt on Chief Massasoit?

Her throat felt as if it were on fire, and her chest felt as if a sharp-toothed knife sawed back and forth. But she couldn't stop. Heedless of the brambles that tore at her skirts, she ran toward the river. She did have an added advantage, though. The messenger was not only overweight but also tired from his long run.

Reaching the river, Merrie slipped off her moccasins and ran along the shore.

All at once a piercing yell stunned her. She whirled about. There was the panting Indian, doggedly chasing after her. She should have remembered that Indians were taught endurance!

Feeling momentary panic, Merrie halted. What should she do? She glanced around for a hiding place. Then, not wasting another minute, she dived in the deep river.

The Indian messenger halted on the bank, his mouth dropping open. Suddenly, he waved his arms and bellowed, "Hey ya! Hey ya!"

Merrie swam to the middle of the river and, taking a deep breath, sank beneath the surface. She knew exactly how she could throw off his pursuit. Surfacing, she yelled and frantically clawed the air.

"Hey ya!" roared the Indian.

Again she went down, and when she surfaced for the second time, she screamed for help. This time she feebly fluttered her hands and sank again. Then she swam beneath the murky water toward a floating clump of vegetation. There, she noiselessly pushed her way to the top of the water and gulped as silently as she could for air. Hiding among the branches, she peered out between the leaves and observed the Indian.

Pacing back and forth, the plump Indian shaded his eyes and squinted up and down the river. Satisfied that she'd drowned, he grunted, then walked away from the shore and into the forest.

For several minutes Merrie remained absolutely still until she was certain the Indian had left. She shuddered when a water snake wriggled smoothly through the water. Then, when all was quiet except for a flock of ducks overhead, she pushed her plastered hair away from her forehead and with long strokes swam to shore.

Wet and frightened, Merrie located her mocccasins and caught her breath enough to move at a fast pace toward home.

Arriving in Plymouth, Merrie hurried down the path. Her damp hair fell in tumbled waves over her shoulders. She wasted no time in rushing to the fields where she knew William Bradford would be with the rest of the men.

When she approached the governor, everyone stopped and stared at her bedraggled appearance. Oliver Loomis, leaning on his hoe, had the biggest eyes of all.

I know what you're thinking, Oliver Loomis, Merrie thought. You're wondering how that young snippet of a Courtland girl dares to rush up to the governor like that! Especially after she's been warned again and again! But little caring what Oliver Loomis thought, she dashed by him. Plymouth was in danger!

"Governor Bradford!" she shouted, breathlessly. "Chief Massasoit is a prisoner of the Narragansets!"

The young governor threw down his hoe. "How do you know this, Mistress Courtland?" he demanded.

She gasped out the story about the Narraganset messenger and the warlike Chief Corbitant. She told how Corbitant might break his alliance with Chief Massasoit and side with the Narragansets.

"Then, we'd better do something about this," William Bradford said firmly. "Men!" he turned to the workers, "I'm calling a council meeting right now!"

Merrie, pleased that he'd taken such swift action, watched as the men stopped weeding and headed for the meetinghouse. Everyone said William Bradford was a more decisive governor than John Carver had been. Now she believed it.

Governor Bradford picked up his hoe, balanced it on his shoulder, and looked at Merrie. "Eat some food and get some rest, Mistress Courtland," he advised. "If your story is true, you will have done a great service to Plymouth."

Later, after Merrie had rested, she asked if she could help Mistress Patience shell peas. Instead Patience insisted Merrie go out and sit in the sun.

Merrie wandered out on the front stoop and noticed Miles Standish drilling his men. She wondered how they'd ever be able to fight hundreds of Indians.

At dusk, when the men had finished marching and musket practice, Zack came by. Looking hot and tired, and still wearing his armor breastplate, he appeared worried.

Taking off his leather-trimmed helmet, Zack wiped his forehead with his arm, his wide-sleeved white shirt fluttering in the breeze. "Captain Miles marched us hard today," he said, adding with a grim smile, "but his lecture on the dangers of an Indian war was even harder to take!"

"I'm afraid there might be an Indian war," she said seriously. "And everyone was so sure we'd have peace because of Chief Massasoit's treaty."

"Well, maybe it isn't true. Perhaps Chief Massasoit is only visiting the Narragansets." Zack sat on the stoop, wearily stretching out his long legs, his mud-caked boots in front of him. "Governor Bradford has sent Squanto and Hobomok to Namasket to see if they can find where the chief is."

"Oh, no," Merrie groaned, leaning against the side of the cabin. "I forgot to tell Governor Bradford that Chief Corbitant hates Squanto. He wants him dead. And now

Squanto's going into Corbitant's village! And with Hobomok!" She thought of Hobomok, Chief Massasoit's special ambassador and translator to Plymouth. Since his arrival, he'd been jealous of Squanto, and the two didn't get along well.

Involuntarily, she reached down, placing her hand on Zack's shoulder. "What will happen to Squanto?" She felt the color drain from her face.

Zack smiled. "Squanto can take care of himself, Merrie."

He held out his hand to her. "Sit down, Merrie, and tell me just what happened at Sowans." He grinned. "From the beginning."

She sank down beside him and briefly told him about Little Fawn's fears. She was even able to laugh at how her pretended drowning had fooled the fat messenger. She rolled her eyes at the end of her story. "When Oliver Loomis saw me after my swim, I knew he'd personally take a whip and drive me out of here."

"Better be careful," Zack admonished, a mocking smile on his lips. "He might hear you." He tipped his head to the left. "Mister Loomis is over by the toolshed, sharpening a scythe."

Merrie quickly glanced up, and sure enough, there was Oliver Loomis, pretending to be absorbed in his task. But Merrie didn't trust him for a minute and was certain that from beneath his brimmed hat, he was secretly watching her.

Zack laughed. "Stop worrying about Oliver Loomis, Merrie. He can't hurt you. Besides, William Bradford was pleased at your courage."

He cocked an eyebrow and gently brushed back a lock of hair. "My little stowaway girl," he said, in a low voice with an amused look on his face. "If I had my way, you'd wear your hair long and flowing every day. When the sun catches the soft curls, it glows like golden daffodils." He leaned closer. "You know," he said, softly, "if Oliver Loomis weren't so close, I'd kiss your rosy cheeks and straight little nose."

Merrie shook her head, smiling. "Don't even think about it. Oliver Loomis would add another of my sins to his growing list."

"Let's go inside," Zack said, standing. "A mug of Mistress Patience's apple cider would taste good. And," he added jocularly, "take your mind off Oliver Loomis!"

She placed both hands in his, gracefully rising to her feet. She wouldn't think about Oliver Loomis for another minute. No matter what happened, she had Zack.

At dusk the next evening, Merrie slowly walked up to the fortified hill, hoping for Squanto's return. But there wasn't a sign of her friend. She leaned against one of the cannons, feeling the summer breeze gently caress her face and hair, and gazed about Plymouth. She longed to be part of the sparkling blue ocean, the sturdy cabins, the tall corn, and the green cedars and pines, but no matter how much she wished for it, she still felt like an outsider.

Suddenly an Indian, his leather-legginged muscles pumping furiously, raced from the fir trees. Her heart leaped. Was it Squanto? She picked up her skirts and hurried down the slope.

Meeting the Indian, Merrie felt her spirits fall. It was Hobomok!

"Hobomok!" she cried, "Wait a minute! Where's Squanto?"

Hobomok slowed and faced her, his dark face glistening with sweat. "He Corbitant's prisoner," he said, gasping for air.

Merrie felt as if her breath had been cut off but hurried to Hobomok's side. "A prisoner?" she asked.

"Yes, I'm going now tell Governor Bradford!"

"Wait," she coaxed, running ahead to the well. "You've run a long way, Hobomok. Let me give you a dipper of cool water."

Hobomok's round face broke into a smile, and he stopped. "Good! I *am* thirsty," he conceded, wiping his brow with his arm. The red paint on his cheeks had trickled down his thick neck in little rivulets, then onto his bare chest, and now smeared his arm.

Greedily he grabbed the tin dipper Merrie offered him. "Squanto and I went to Namasket, Corbitant's village," he said, drinking noisily. "Chief Corbitant threw us in a hut, with guards standing by the door." He wiped his dripping mouth, smudging the red dye even more.

"Oh, Hobomok," Merrie said, biting her lip. "What happened?"

"I escaped. Corbitant dragged me and Squanto from the house this morning, saying he will kill us both!" He paused dramatically. "He held a big knife to my throat." His hand flashed across his neck. "He says if Squanto die, then English 'lose their tongue.'"

"But you got away and Squanto didn't?" she persisted, confused.

"I fought. I kicked. I ran from the guards."

"And Squanto?" she whispered.

Hobomok shrugged. "He maybe dead by now."

"Oh, no," she said, feeling a dull aching sorrow steal over her.

"Corbitant is a bad man," Hobomok said angrily. "Chief Bradford must know!"

"And did you find out where Chief Massasoit is?" Merrie asked. But Hobomok had already sprinted away, heading for the fields.

Merrie sank down on the wooden bench, staring at the vine-covered well, but only the image of Squanto's friendly face danced before her. She buried her face in her hands. If Squanto was dead, war would be declared. And war meant the end of Plymouth!

Chapter
Twenty-one

IT had been three days since ten armed men, including Zack, had marched to Namasket, Corbitant's village. Under the command of Miles Standish they had left on a rainy August 3rd. The captain had ordered his men to kill Corbitant if Squanto was found dead.

Everyone knew how grave the situation was. They didn't know whether to expect the safe return of Miles Standish's men or face an Indian attack.

On the fourth day Merrie was gathering blueberries near Allerton's Cove when she heard the drumbeat of Standish's marching men. With her basket only half full, she dashed back to the village, where all the settlers, no matter what they had been doing, were out in force to welcome the soldiers back. Now, at last, she'd hear what had happened.

Zack, tall and flushed with victory, immediately found Merrie standing in front of her cabin. Oblivious of Mistress Patience and everyone else, even Oliver Loomis, he swept her into his arms as if he were about to kiss her.

"Zack!' she gasped, glimpsing Oliver Loomis's cold stare. Her cheeks stained scarlet. Turning back to Zack, she said happily, "You must have good news." Then her smile vanished when she glanced nervously at Oliver Loomis. "Let's go inside."

"I do have good news," Zack exclaimed, leaning his musket by the door. "We did it!" he said triumphantly, his even teeth flashing white against his dark face.

"And Squanto?" she asked, her heartbeat accelerating.

"He's safe, my love," he said, tossing his helmet on the table and sitting in front of the empty fireplace. "Right now, he's talking to Governor Bradford. You'll see Squanto soon."

"Oh, Zack, I was so worried. Please," she said, hurrying to pour him a cup of ale, "I want to hear everything!"

Zack took a sip from the pewter cup she'd handed him. "You should have seen Captain Standish! Miles didn't back down for a minute. First he commanded us to fire our muskets. Then we marched into Namasket. All the Indian braves threw their bows and arrows at Standish's feet and promised allegiance to him."

"Did Chief Corbitant, too?" Merrie questioned, refilling Zack's cup.

"He ran away, but Miles made a strong speech to the Indians, telling them there was no place for Corbitant to hide. And," Zack continued, "if he threatened Plymouth and dared mock Chief Massasoit's peace, he'd be tracked to the ends of the earth and killed."

"There will be peace," she said softly, her dark eyes sparkling with joy.

"Thanks to you, Merrie," he said, reaching over and taking her hand. "If it hadn't been for your warning, we wouldn't have known about Corbitant's plan to attack. You've more than proved your value, 'stowaway girl.'"

"I hope Corbitant's found," she said. "If he had killed Squanto . . ." her voice trailed off grimly.

"Then, we wouldn't have had such a happy ending," Zack said levelly.

Their eyes met. She knew what he meant. Even though Captain Standish's speech was daring, he and his twenty-two armed men were no match for an entire Indian tribe.

In the next few days Chief Massasoit returned safely from the Narragansets, where he had been cementing good relations. Also Chief Corbitant humbly went to Massasoit and asked for his help in making peace with Plymouth.

The colony was again safe, and Merrie breathed a sigh of relief. Life was good, and at the end of August the rich crops were ready to be harvested.

October came, and as Merrie spread a quilt over the fence for airing, she marveled still at how lucky she was. It was a golden day. She and Zack were in love, and she knew their futures were inextricably bound together. Plymouth was secure, and she had a wonderful sister in Little Fawn and a sweet mother in Mistress Patience. Even though some of the settlers were wary and the Elders watched her more than she was comfortable with, she still felt as if she were earning a niche here. In a low voice, she sang a lilting melody while she thought of Zack:

"The sound of thy sweet name, my dearest
    treasure,
Delights me more than sight of other faces:
A glimpse of thy sweet face breeds me more
    pleasure
Than any other's kindest words and graces."

A shadow fell across the grass, causing her to glance up. When she saw Oliver Loomis, she froze. "What is it?" she asked, staring into his thin face.

"Still singing evil love songs," he said, his ice-gray eyes boring into hers. "I believe the Elders have warned you once about such singing," he said.

"It's — it's only an English song I know," she said weakly.

He said smoothly, "Of course — my dear." He sat on a stump and clasped his bony fingers over one knee, observing her.

"What is it?" she repeated, trying to remain calm. Whenever Oliver Loomis wanted to speak to her, it was always bad news.

"Zachariah has quite a cache of furs accumulated," he said silkily, "and should be able to make a sizable profit on his shipment. Any day now a ship is due into Plymouth Harbor."

"Yes," she agreed, "Zack is a good trapper." What was he leading up to?

"Zachariah is well liked by everyone here," Oliver Loomis said, tipping back his wide-brimmed hat. "He's a good worker and has a fine reputation. No one has a better standing in the colony than young Zachariah Gaines."

"I know," she said, puzzled. Obviously he was getting to the point, but what was it?

"It seems to me," he continued smoothly, "that you prefer the Indians to the colonists." He studied her face. "I'm certain the Wampanoags and your blood sister would welcome you at Sowans," he said the words sneeringly.

"Yes," she said evenly, "Chief Massasoit is my friend."

"Indians!" His lip curled disdainfully. "They could attack anytime! Treaties mean nothing to them."

"That's not true!" she cried.

"Watch who you're speaking to!" he hissed. "You forget yourself! You don't know the meaning of the words humility or humbleness! Well," he continued smugly, "you have a long list of transgressions, and I intend to see that the Council receives them. You sleep during Elder Brewster's sermons, you run back and forth between Sowans and Plymouth, and you sing immoral songs! We don't have room for someone who flaunts herself as you do! Zachariah hurts only himself by being seen with you, Mistress Merrie Courtland!"

"That's not true!" she said, flushing angrily and boldly meeting his cold eyes. She kept her head high, not wanting him to realize the misery his words caused.

"Oh, isn't it? Right now, Zachariah Gaines is being considered for the governing board. But as long as you're at his side, he won't stand a chance. In fact," he added, his expression grim, "I doubt if Zachariah will ever be a respected member of this community." He shook his head. "It's too bad. Why would you want to hurt him?"

"I-I don't," she stammered.

"If I were you," Oliver Loomis said, lifting a bony finger to point at her, "I'd be on the next boat to England or go and live with my Indian friends." He turned and left her standing speechless by the vegetable patch.

Wearily she swept off her white cap, staring at the lace edges. She had tried so hard to fit in — even wearing a cap and doing up her hair. Oh, what was the use, she thought, as she furiously loosened her hair, letting it fall down her back.

Tears stung her eyes and slowly trickled down her cheeks. Whatever she did was wrong, wrong. She'd never leave Plymouth because of Oliver Loomis, but if she thought for one minute she was hurting Zack, she'd leave on the next boat!

Merrie strode down the path and out of Plymouth. Once outside the gate, she broke into a run. Little Fawn said she'd be swimming at the river every afternoon until it turned cold. She had to talk to her. Little Fawn always seemed to handle things calmly. And she helped Merrie see things in a different light.

As she ran along the trail, she thought of Oliver Loomis's remarks about the Indians! Why did he hate them? If it hadn't been for Squanto, the Pilgrims would never have survived the winter. But it seemed Oliver Loomis hated everyone who was good and helpful, especially those who didn't sit in the front row of the meetinghouse and have their eyes riveted on Elder Brewster! Well, perhaps it would be better to leave. Only this time she wouldn't tell anyone her plans — not even Little Fawn.

Approaching the river bend, where the graceful willow branches drooped into the turquoise waters, she heard laughter and splashing water. Fierce Falcon, playing water tag with a friend, stopped and waved to Merrie as she came into sight. Little Fawn, stretched out on a flat rock that jutted over the water, had her face lifted to the sun, and her slim, supple body was relaxed.

Climbing up on the rock next to her, Merrie

said, "I-I had to get away." She settled herself alongside Little Fawn.

"What wrong?" Little Fawn asked.

"Oh, it's the usual," she answered, managing a tight little smile.

"Oliver Loomis," guessed Little Fawn.

"Oliver Loomis," Merrie repeated grimly. Suddenly she lashed out. "I hate him, Little Fawn — I hate him!" She slapped the rock so hard her palm smarted. "He told me I'm hurting Zack just by being near him."

Little Fawn laughed huskily. "That not true. Everyone like Merrie Yellow-Hair!"

"The Indians like me," Merrie said, smiling at Little Fawn. Then she sadly shook her head. "But not all the Pilgrims do, I'm afraid."

Merrie lay back in the sun and closed her eyes wearily, trying to forget Oliver Loomis's words.

Chapter
Twenty-two

IN mid-October of 1621, Governor Bradford proclaimed a feast day for the Pilgrims. They had a lot to be thankful for. They had survived a stormy voyage, were at peace with the Indians, had plenty to eat, and the sickness was over. Also, land had been cleared, cabins built, and more planned, but the most important reason for thanks was that they'd accomplished what they'd set out to do: established a colony where they could worship in freedom.

The Pilgrims joyfully agreed with Bradford's "day of thanks" and set about to plan a lavish feast. They gathered food, got the provisions Captain Jones had left for them from the *Mayflower*'s stores — salt beef, salt pork, butter, and biscuits — and the women immediately set about baking and preparing corn puddings.

Merrie had to get away from the frenzied,

happy activity. As an excuse she told Mistress Patience she'd pick a basketful of wild grapes. A dark and sinking feeling had come over her when she realized she'd soon be leaving for England. The settlers expected a provisions ship any day.

She took a deep, ragged breath. If her love for Zack had pulled her off the *Mayflower* once, this time her love for him would drive her away forever.

Merrie strolled past the wild cranberry bogs, enjoying the warm sun. Fall days were warm and sunny, but the nights were chilly, which meant an early winter. But not for her, she thought bitterly. Her winter would be in London — away from Zack. Well, he'd be better off without her. She wouldn't stand in the way of his becoming a respected leader of the community, and knowing Zack, she had no doubt he would be. His place was here, at Plymouth. Tears blinded her. How strong his love was! If Zack knew, he'd follow her anywhere. Well, he'd never learn her secret plan.

The deep crimson cranberries, stretched across the marshy land, lifted her spirits a little. The green hills were ablaze with late blooms in blues and scarlets. And the maple and oak leaves, a riot of orange, gold, and crimson, turned the countryside into a brilliant patchwork quilt, edged by the sapphire blue of the ocean.

The best thing about the coming feast, Merrie thought as she sat on the grass, was the invitation extended to her Indian friends.

For an hour she sat on the soft ground, plucking aimlessly at the pine needles surrounding her and reliving the first time she'd seen Zack. A low moan caught in her throat. How could she bear to leave him?

Then her thoughts turned to Luke. Would he be true to his word and sail into Plymouth harbor on the next ship? The image of his happy grin, red hair, broad shoulders, and freewheeling sailor's gait brought a smile to her lips. She missed Luke's open friendliness — so different from the Pilgrims. Their first meeting, though, hadn't been very friendly. The memory of how she'd hidden in the long boat and Luke's discovery of her came back in startling clarity. How long ago that seemed!

The lengthening shadows reminded her it was late, and she jumped up. She hadn't picked one grape. In a flurried rush, she ran to where the thick vines grew and began to grab whole bunches.

When she returned at dusk, candles already shone through the paper-covered cabin windows.

She hurried into the house and put the grapes on the table. Mistress Patience looked up from scraping carrots, letting the bowl rest in her lap. "I'm glad you're back, Merrie," she said calmly. "I don't want you in the woods at dark."

The fire felt good, and Merrie warmed her

hands before the flames. "I don't want to be out there, either," she said with a slight shiver, "not with prowling wolves."

Mistress Patience informed her that the men had set up the trestle tables under the big oaks for Friday's feast. "It will be a grand day," she said. "The corn is all picked, but it's too bad the six acres of English barley and peas came to nothing."

"And if it hadn't been for the Indians," Merrie said, "we wouldn't even have had the corn."

"I know, dear," Mistress Patience agreed. "Everyone realizes how much we owe the Indians. That's why Governor Bradford sent Squanto to invite them."

"Is he back yet?"

"No, tomorrow," Mistress Patience said, with a laugh. "He's as happy as a bee buzzing between Plymouth and Sowans. You'd think he planned the whole celebration."

Merrie smiled. "May I help?" She looked proudly at the fat carrots from their garden.

"Well," Mistress Patience hesitated, looking at Merrie's purple-stained fingers. "I think you've done enough already."

"No, I haven't," Merrie countered honestly. "I wasted most of the afternoon."

A flicker of a smile crossed Patience's face. "And how did you waste it?"

"Oh," Merrie said casually, "daydreaming." Mistress Patience would never realize that her "daydream" was really a "nightmare"! She studied Mistress Patience's sweet heart-shaped face and wished she didn't have to leave her alone. She wondered if Mistress Patience would understand why she had left. Perhaps she would. Someday.

"I know there's something I can do with the big day so close," Merrie urged. "Give me a task."

"If you really want to, you can peel onions."

"I'd love to," Merrie said with a grin. "I'm an expert at peeling onions."

Mistress Patience raised her brows. "You are?"

"Yes," Merrie answered, laughing. "That was one of my first tasks on board ship. Mistress Hopkins was quite disgusted with me and said I peeled half the onion away! But I learned!" Today, she thought, everything reminded her of the *Mayflower* voyage. She was different since those ship days. She had learned much more than how to peel an onion.

As Merrie peeled off the first onion skin, she wondered what Nancy Bates would think if she could see her now. Callused hands. Clothes all ragged. She glanced at Mistress Patience. Her dark dress was tattered and patched, too. That's why everyone eagerly waited for the next ship and the supplies. Everyone, that is, except her. Merrie bent her head. It wasn't just the onions that made her eyes water and burn, and she was glad she had something to do.

Later that night, exhausted, she crawled into bed. Tomorrow was the last day of preparation before the Indians would arrive on

Friday. Little Fawn was coming tomorrow afternoon and would spend the night. Merrie stared into the blackness, tossing and turning. She was so tired, yet sleep wouldn't come.

Then it was morning, and Merrie was being awakened by the scraping of chairs across the floor. Zack had come to carry them to the feast. She burrowed under the covers, pretending to be asleep. The less she saw of Zack, the easier it would be to leave him.

Zack, carrying four chairs, said to Mistress Patience, "Is Merrie going to sleep all day?"

Mistress Patience chuckled softly. "She's always up at dawn with me. Let her sleep for a change."

Zack stood at the door. "I'm going hunting with Miles Standish. Tell Merrie I'll be gone all day. We'll bring back plenty of turkeys and geese for the fire."

"We'll need them," Mistress Patience responded warmly. "We can count on fifty settlers but don't know how many Indians to expect." She stood at the door with Zack.

Zack's rich laughter filled the room. "I've heard that Chief Massasoit might bring his whole village!"

Mistress Patience groaned. "Mercy, whatever will we do! Merrie and I had better pick more pumpkins."

After the door closed, Merrie sat up, rubbing her eyes.

"You missed seeing Zack," Mistress Patience said, glancing at her.

"I did?" Merrie asked innocently. She

threw off the covers, sat on the edge of her bunk, and stretched. "Little Fawn comes today," she said with a smile of anticipation.

"Yes, and we've a lot to do before she gets here," Mistress Patience said briskly, taking a steaming johnnycake out of the pan and putting it on Merrie's plate. "We need to clean oysters and clams."

"I'll do it," Merrie volunteered. She wanted to keep busy so she wouldn't have to think.

"Two buckets of clams are on the stoop. While you're doing that, I'll mix the succotash."

"Hmmm," Merrie said, moistening her lips. "That will taste good!" She loved the rich stew of meat pieces and corn that Squanto had taught them to make.

Merrie worked all day. She picked turnips, cucumbers, and cabbages, then gathered eggs. By afternoon she was tired, and when she saw Little Fawn's slim form swinging confidently down the lane, she was ready for a cool cup of apple cider.

"Little Fawn!" Merrie called. "Come in." She poured two cups of cider. Little Fawn looked beautiful in her deeply fringed leather dress and beaded green belt, with an elaborate shell necklace, dyed green, blue, and lavender, about her slender neck.

The two girls talked until late afternoon when Mistress Patience came in and gave each a basket with a request to fill them with berries.

With baskets on their arms, the girls

strolled by the large pits the men had dug for tomorrow's cooking fires and walked on past the oak grove where the wooden tables were set up.

Merrie's happiness felt as warm and as sad as this last day of autumn. Soon, too, her contented glow would wane and fade.

The girls chattered, happily picking gooseberries until their baskets brimmed.

Coming back to Plymouth, they sat at one of the long outdoor tables, and Merrie tossed a gooseberry into her mouth. "Ugh. Too sour," she said, grimacing.

Little Fawn laughed. "Gooseberries taste better baked. There will be lots of food for feast. Tomorrow will be fun." Merrie laughed, too.

"What is everyone doing?" Little Fawn asked, looking with astonishment as Pilgrims darted back and forth.

"The men over there," Merrie said, pointing at a group, "are laying out a racecourse. They've planned other games, too, like Spoon Ball."

"Games!" Little Fawn said gleefully, clapping her hands. "I cannot wait! Maybe we will teach you our moccasin game."

"Moccasin game?" asked Merrie curiously. "What's that?"

Little Fawn lithely leaned down, slipped off her moccasins, and placed them on the table. "Merrie," she ordered. "Put your moccasins on the table." Then, searching the ground, she picked up four acorns and a long stick.

"What. . . ?"

"Wait," Little Fawn said, smiling impishly and handing Merrie the stick.

Next she notched one acorn with her knife before placing it with the other three under each of the moccasins. She stopped and explained, "Braves play this game. They have two teams, three men on side. We beat drums, and people sing."

"Sorry," Merrie teased. "I don't have a drum, and," she lowered her voice, "I don't dare sing."

Little Fawn continued, "A big crowd gathers to watch the game." Her face lit with a smile. "I'll show you how to play." Rapidly she changed the position of the moccasins. "Now," she said, settling back, "you point with the stick at the moccasin that hides the notched acorn." With arms folded, she watched Merrie, a secretive smile on her face.

Merrie, enjoying the game, pointed to the third moccasin.

Little Fawn peeked under the moccasin and then triumphantly drew out an unmarked acorn. "You lose," she said, laughing. "When the men play, they give up part of their clothing: feathers, headdress, vest, and, sometimes," she giggled, "they play until only they wear breechcloth."

"Let's try again," Merrie said excitedly. "This time you won't fool me."

"We see," Little Fawn said slyly, as she deftly moved the moccasins about.

Suddenly there was a roar, and Oliver Loomis stormed up to the table. With a sweep of his long arm, he scattered moccasins and acorns, sending them flying into the air.

Horrified, Merrie leaped to her feet as Oliver Loomis viciously shoved Little Fawn to the ground.

Blinking, the Indian maid lay amid shoes and acorns, warily watching this strange, tall man all dressed in black.

Oliver Loomis, fury almost choking him, shouted hoarsely, "Don't bring your gambling Indian games to Plymouth!" He shook his fist furiously in the air.

Merrie rushed to help Little Fawn to her feet. Then, her brown eyes blazing, she spun about to confront Oliver Loomis. "How dare you touch Little Fawn!" she shouted, pale with anger. "She's a guest here!"

"Don't ever talk to me that way!" Oliver Loomis said between clenched teeth. He hovered above her like a glowering scarecrow. "I will take no more from you, Merrie Courtland! This feast is the last meal you will eat with the Saints!"

Suddenly, he grabbed her shoulders and shook her violently.

Stunned, Merrie stumbled backward. Her head rang from his harsh words, but more than anything she was sick with rage and humiliation. If she could, she'd leave Plymouth this minute!

Chapter
Twenty-three

AFTER snarling Oliver Loomis had stomped away, both Little Fawn and Merrie were too stunned to move. They talked in hushed tones as they soberly slipped on their moccasins.

After they were in bed, they continued talking about Loomis. "He is a bad man," Little Fawn whispered, not wanting Mistress Patience to overhear. "With a big temper."

Merrie shivered, pulling the quilt around her shoulders. "Now you know how much he hates me," she said, still feeling his punishing hands wrenching her shoulders.

"Are you going to tell Chief Bradford?" Little Fawn questioned.

"No," she murmured. "It's no use telling the governor, Little Fawn. He listens to Oliver Loomis. All the Elders do."

"But he threatened you! Pushed me to ground!" Little Fawn said in a low voice choked with indignation. "It is not right!"

"I know it, Little Fawn, but he's a respected Saint, and I'm nothing but a 'stow-away girl.' "

They talked far into the night, and the longer they talked, the stronger Merrie's resolve was to leave. It was better for Zack, better for Mistress Patience, and better for everyone.

Merrie turned and faced the wall. She shuddered to think what would happen if Zack found out. A major fight over her was the last thing she wanted.

The next day Merrie and Little Fawn helped Mistress Patience carry huge baskets of plums, strawberries, gooseberries, huckle-berries, and blackberries to the tables. They had sweetened the fruit with wild honey for the dessert.

All at once Chief Massasoit and his people appeared. Governor Bradford hurried to wel-come them, but the women hung back, shoot-ing nervous looks at one another. "Oh, no," Merrie whispered to Mistress Patience, "we can't possibly stretch the food for this many Indians! There must be a hundred!"

Fortunately Chief Massasoit caught the women's panic-stricken glances, surveyed the tables, then nodded wisely. Immediately he ordered several warriors off to a hunt.

"Let the games begin!" announced William Bradford.

Merrie and Little Fawn hurried to the sea-shore to watch the racing and jumping con-tests. Targets had been set up, and Indian warriors challenged some of the Pilgrims to a bow and arrow match.

Everyone was shouting and laughing. Merrie forgot about Oliver Loomis and enjoyed the sound of squealing children and exuberant voices. It had been a long, sad winter, and the Pilgrims hadn't had one holiday. Since they didn't believe in religious holidays, they'd even worked on Christmas Day, Merrie remembered bitterly. Well, today Saints and Strangers alike were ready to share a joyful day.

The mischievous Billington boys threw a stool ball back and forth. This time, Merrie thought, no one could get hurt — not with a ball stuffed with feathers!

Zack motioned Merrie to come and watch him in an arm-wrestling contest. He introduced her to a tall, muscular Indian named Blue Corn. The men strained and groaned as their locked arms went first to the left, then to the right. At last Blue Corn, veins bulging on his forehead, and with a grunt of satisfaction, forced Zack's hand down on the flat rock.

Zack shrugged and grinned at Merrie, rising to his feet with an easy grace. He reached for his musket. "Before I go to the target shoot," he said, his dark curling hair ruffling in the breeze, "will you save a place for me at the table?"

"Yes," she promised, her eyes sparkling with affection. "Good luck." Her voice was filled with pride as she watched him stride away. In the distance she noticed the hunters return and give the women five deer. Their hunt had been successful, and now so would be their dinner.

Suddenly, Miles Standish led a parade of men all around the shore. Trumpets blared, and the drummer beat a sharp rat-a-tat.

Little Fawn tugged at Merrie's sleeve. "Let's join the parade!"

"Let's!" Merrie responded happily, feeling the drumbeat down to her toes. They fell in behind the men, lifting their feet high to the rhythm of the music.

After the parade Miles Standish, who had chosen his best men, with Zack in the forefront, led them in a smart display of military maneuvers.

Merrie turned to Little Fawn and said, "We'd better go back and help with the food." She'd been lucky to have spent the day with Little Fawn. But the women had insisted. Since Merrie was the only one with an Indian guest, they said, she should be freed of responsibilities to entertain Little Fawn, so that the two girls had very little work to do and more time for fun.

"Race you!" Little Fawn shouted, and was off and running.

Merrie, lifting her skirts, dashed after her. Little Fawn lithely sprinted ahead, her long brown legs moving with ease. But Merrie, unleashing a spurt of energy, soon caught up with her. Together they ran side by side.

Panting and laughing they came to a halt at the first table. Little Fawn hugged Merrie with delight. "You are a good runner," she said admiringly.

They smelled the savory stews and puddings laid out before them. Scanning the long table laden with food, Merrie gasped. She had never seen such a wonderful display of delicacies — not even in London. Venison, turkey, eel pie, wild plums, were all there. Mounds of boiled cabbage, turnips, parsnips, beets, and onions steamed in huge pots. Two large fish, one a roasted bass and the other a baked salmon, were decorated with raw radishes and cucumbers.

Surrounding them were huge fires containing open spits on which deer, duck, and geese slowly turned. Lobsters and oysters roasted over beds of hot coals. And there were mountains of corn. Parched. Boiled. Roasted ears. Hoecakes. Ashcakes. Succotash. Corn pudding. Even white, fluffy popcorn was ready to be eaten. Some of the baskets of popped corn had maple syrup drizzled over the top, a tasty treat they had learned from Squanto.

Squanto, looking handsome in his leather leggings and leather tunic, approached the girls. His wide-brimmed Pilgrim hat was the only thing that set him apart from the other Indian guests. But Squanto, without a doubt, belonged here! "You like?" he asked, pushing back his hat and openly pleased at the lavish display.

"It's beautiful," Merrie answered breathlessly.

"Come, Merrie," Squanto said. "I will show you something." He motioned to Little Fawn, too. Moving proudly to another table where all kinds of fruits were prepared, he pointed. "I showed the women how to dry fruit and bake in dough cases," he said, puffing out his chest.

"Hmmm," she said, smiling. "Squanto, you're the best cook here." She leaned down, smelling the delectable cherries surrounded by baked dough.

Large pitchers of both white and red wine were placed at each end of the table. Merrie was pleased. The wild grapes she'd helped pick made fine wine.

Squanto grinned at her. "We will eat soon, I hope."

Mistress Patience, a wooden ladle in her hand, joined them. "We're almost ready to eat," she said. "Master Squanto, would you be so kind as to take the kettles of venison stew and clam chowder off the fire? Put them on the table by the big oak."

"I am glad to, Mistress Sedgewick," Squanto said.

"Then, when Captain Standish's men march into this clearing," she said, "we begin our feast." She smiled at Merrie, lightly touching her cheek. Then she did the same with Little Fawn. "My two darling girls," she said softly. Turning away, she went back to supervise Edward Winslow and John

Howland, who were carving up a deer carcass and placing the sliced venison on a nearby platter.

In a few minutes Standish's men marched briskly down Main Street and into the clearing.

"Ready!" Captain Standish barked, his hair and beard blazing red-gold in the afternoon sun. "Aim!" He held his sword stiffly in front of his perspiring face. "Fire!" he roared.

The men pointed their muskets at the sky, and the volley echoed from hill to hill. Chief Massasoit, startled, lifted his hand in dismay, but when he saw it was only a show, he relaxed and laughed with the others.

Captain Standish, the ruff about his stubby neck sparkling white, nodded to one of his men. Together they climbed to the top of Fort Hill. All at once one of the cannons were fired. BOOM! The resounding cannonball made a tremendous noise.

The astounded Indians jumped back.

However, Chief Massasoit soon recovered his usual stoic calm. "I glad colonists my friend. Narragansets better watch out!" Laughter greeted his words.

Merrie glanced about at the families she knew. Mistress Hopkins was with her children, and Stephen, her husband, was walking toward her. They were one of the few families that hadn't been devastated by the general sickness, except their baby, Oceanus, the only child born on the *Mayflower*'s voyage, who had died. Constanta Hopkins, whom Merrie had shared a berth with, was friendly, but in the past months all of them had been so busy they hadn't had time to keep up their friendship. Or maybe Constanta, like everyone else, didn't want to keep it up.

All at once the Allertons and Brewsters broke into song, singing one of the hymns William Brewster had composed. Merrie rather liked this one because the words had a special meaning:

> In wilderness He did me guide.
> And in strange lands for me provide.
> In fears and wants, through weal and woe,
> A Pilgrim passed I to and fro.

Merrie glanced over at the bench where John Alden and Priscilla Mullins held hands. John whispered in Priscilla's ear. Was he proposing to her, Merrie wondered. She sighed, thinking how happy they looked.

Susanna White and her new husband, Edward Winslow, walked on either side of Peregrine, holding onto his pudgy little arms as he toddled between them. Peregrine was almost a year old now. What a future the little boy had ahead of him, Merrie thought. Then her reverie was broken.

All eyes fastened on Mary Brewster, who had climbed up on a wooden bench. "The feast," she paused dramatically, waving a spoon overhead, "is ready!" No one wasted any time in getting seated. Most of the

Indians, however, preferred sitting on the ground.

Zack broke out of Captain Standish's marching formation and hurried to Merrie's side.

At the table, Merrie sat between Zack and Little Fawn. Elder Brewster offered a brief prayer of thanksgiving while Merrie silently offered her own thanks. She felt love and an inner delight on this special warm October evening. She was with friends. It had been a hard year, but it was worth every day!

Governor Bradford, a tankard of wine lifted, cried in a jovial voice, "Let the eating begin!"

The day had been wonderful, and as Merrie cut her roast turkey, she felt a peace and serenity that would last a lifetime of memories. She planned to enjoy her last few weeks at Plymouth and wouldn't think about her future across the Atlantic. Not, at least, until she was on the boat.

As she took her first mouthful, she glanced up and saw Oliver Loomis coldly observing her.

The food in her mouth turned to ashes, and she put down her spoon. By the smirk on his face, he was obviously relishing her discomfort. She was unable to eat another bite.

Chapter
Twenty-four

MERRIE sat at the table, her slender fingers tensed in her lap. She was no longer hungry. Oliver Loomis's sneer had spoiled her festive mood.

"Merrie," Zack said, offering her hot bread steaming from the oven, "you're not eating. Anything wrong?"

"N-nothing," she stammered, wishing she could bolt from this place and run into the woods.

"Eat some corn pudding?" he urged, passing her a brimming bowl of the rich corn and syrup.

Miserably, she shook her head.

"Come on, 'stowaway girl,'" he teased, reaching for a fruit basket. "Surely you'll eat some dried strawberries."

When she didn't respond, he said with concern, "Tell me, Merrie, what's wrong? This is supposed to be a happy day." He touched her nose with his finger. "No sad faces allowed!"

His look of love sent an aching hurt through her. She closed her eyes against the suffocating tightness in her throat.

The laughter at the table and the friendly banter made her realize what an outsider she was. The name "stowaway girl" rang in her ears. That's what she'd always be, and no amount of lighthearted teasing could alter that.

Zack rose to his feet, a wide smile on his face, and lifted his cup to Squanto at the end of the table. "To Squanto!" he said. "For all his help these past months."

Everyone lifted cups. "Here! Here! To Squanto! Our friend!"

Merrie woodenly held up her cup but couldn't bring herself to drink. Her stomach was twisted and knotted. She bit her lip, and perspiration sprang to her forehead. She had to escape! She jumped to her feet.

Startled, Zack looked up at her. "Merrie," he said in a low voice, "please, sit down." Gently he took her arm. "Chief Massasoit is about to speak. Don't insult him by leaving."

Desolate, she sank down again, staring at her plate. How could she sit through more toasts of friendship and laughter?

The majestic chief stood, his magnificent feathered headdress and soft leather suit golden in the sunset. His eyes roved from the faces of the Indians to the colonists.

"There," the regal chief said, pointing

dramatically, "is the person who symbolizes the closeness of Indian and white." His English was halting but clear, and his voice rang when he announced "Merrie Courtland!"

At the mention of her name, Merrie's head jerked up. Bewildered, she stared at the chief.

"This girl," the chief continued, "comes to Sowans. She has more than a friend in Little Fawn. They are blood sisters. Merrie ran from Sowans to Plymouth to warn you of Chief Corbitant. She was chased by a Namasket messenger, but it did not stop her. She loves Plymouth. She loves her people — and her friends." He touched his chest lightly.

Many surprised faces turned in Merrie's direction with murmurs of approval.

Embarrassed, Merrie smiled, feeling a warm swell of pride rise within her. She hadn't wanted everyone to know about Little Fawn and how she was chased through the forest by the messenger, but now that the chief had told, she found she was pleased people knew. But she also felt guilty at her pride. A little voice inside repeated the words she'd heard last Sunday at the meetinghouse, "Pride goeth before a fall." She looked down at her folded hands. She had done what she had to and didn't expect such praise from the chief of the Wampanoags. When she remembered the people who had lost family members this past winter, her accomplishments were small and insignificant. She glanced at Oliver Loomis, whose mouth had formed a big O of shock.

She looked away, pleased. For once he was the one who was suffering discomfort.

"Merrie Courtland! Come forward!" the chief ordered imperiously. But he smiled, and his eyes shone.

Merrie paused. Her heart hammered, and her legs felt weak.

"Merrie," Mistress Patience urged, leaning across the table, "go up to the head table. The chief is waiting."

Zack gave her hand a quick, reassuring squeeze as she slowly rose and walked hesitantly toward the chief. How could she, Merrie Courtland, a stowaway girl, receive such a glowing tribute? I must be dreaming, she thought as she heard John Alden say loudly, "Brave girl!"

Someone else called out, "Good for you, Mistress Merrie. We're proud of you!"

Susanna White Winslow leaned forward, catching at Merrie's sleeve. "You're wonderful," she said, smiling radiantly.

As Merrie stood alongside Chief Massasoit, her mouth was so dry she couldn't swallow. She hoped she wouldn't have to say anything.

Chief Massasoit looked down at her, holding a beaded headband with two red feathers. "This," he said, "is for you, Merrie Courtland. You are now an honored member of the Wampanoag tribe!"

As the chief solemnly fitted the headband over her thick hair, Merrie felt hot blood rush to her face, reddening her cheeks. But she couldn't hide her delight or her sparkling eyes when she murmured, "Thank you, Chief Massasoit."

"Say something to the audience," the chief said.

Shyly she turned, facing the crowd. "I-I accept this headband with gratitude," she said, the words catching in her throat. "It's made this day of thanks very special for me."

Governor Bradford rose. "I propose another toast. To Mistress Merrie Courtland," he said. "We're glad she stowed away on the *Mayflower* and became part of our colony!"

Merrie, tears shimmering in her eyes, gazed about, her heart bursting with joy as the Pilgrims slowly rose and lifted their cups to her.

Returning to her place, she looked into Zack's eyes. For the first time she realized she might be able to stay after all. Zack reached for her hand and smiled broadly. "I'm proud of you, my stowaway girl." His voice was husky with feeling.

Mistress Patience came and hugged Merrie's shoulders. "I'm lucky to have you for a daughter." She stepped back as Mary Brewster and others crowded around Merrie.

Looking at Zack and Little Fawn, Merrie smiled, and her brown eyes glowed. Had Chief Massasoit changed her future in a five-minute speech? It didn't occur to her that her own stubborn courage had earned that speech. She felt the pats on her back and heard the friendly words, but she couldn't absorb what had happened.

She was so involved in trying to sort out her feelings that she didn't see Oliver Loomis until he stood before her. She nervously glanced about, but everyone else seemed to have left. With his hands clasped behind his back and the usual glower on his face, he said coldly, "It seems you've won the settlers' approval, Mistress Courtland. I don't agree with Governor Bradford's sentiments, but . . ." — his back went rigid — "I do wish to ask your pardon for any pain I may have caused you." He hesitated. "Or your friend Little Fawn."

Merrie was too thunderstruck to reply. She could only gaze into his haughty face. Finally, she realized why he had apologized. He was afraid she would inform the Elders about his threats, his shaking her, and his treatment of Little Fawn. He was afraid for himself.

Well, she wouldn't throw his apology back in his face, no matter how reluctantly he gave it. Instead, she looked at him and wondered, from habit, what he thought of her half-Indian, half-colonial garb. Her hand strayed to her headdress, and she was dismayed to find it at a rakish angle. It must have happened when she was jostled by everyone coming up to her after the chief's speech. Her hair, too, so neatly done up this morning, had loosened and framed her face with long wisps of golden tendrils. She tried to tuck it back, but it was no use.

Oliver Loomis pursed his thin lips and shook his head as if to say, "You'll never change, Merrie Courtland."

Pretending not to understand his disapproving look, she dropped her hand and said evenly, with a slight smile of defiance, "Everything between us is forgotten, Master Loomis."

A yellow light flickered in his gray hawk-like eyes, and for a moment he faltered. "I thank you, Mistress Courtland," then added dryly, "I don't think we can ever be friends, but at least I'll make an attempt to tolerate your wild ways."

"That's all I ask," Merrie murmured. Then she lifted her chin and said pleasantly, "Now if you'll excuse me, I see Zack is waiting for me."

Bowing slightly, Oliver Loomis turned on his heels and with stiff dignity walked away.

For a moment Merrie watched him leave. Then with her heart singing, she hurried to meet Zack, who waited for her by the old oak.

Zack watched her with delight as she swung down the lane with easy grace toward him. "I've been watching you and Oliver Loomis," he said. "Has he insulted you again?" His black brows drew together in a frown.

"Everything is fine, Zack," she said. Her eyes shone. "Very fine."

He grinned down at her. "Will you walk by the seashore with me?"

"I'd be honored, sir," she said, taking his arm and heading for the beach.

As they walked along under the last purple rays of the dying sun, Merrie had never known such blissful happiness, especially when Zack took her hand.

"The provision ship should be in this week," Zack said. "Hope they bring some livestock. I'm thirsty for a cup of cool fresh milk! Also," he added throwing back his slim shoulders, "I'll be able to send back sixty prime beaver pelts."

"Zack, you've done well here." If he was proud of her, she was equally proud of him. Thank goodness it was his beaver furs going back to England, and not herself. Now her love for Zack could not hurt him. She was a member of the colony in her own right, accepted for herself.

The surf made a gentle soughing sound against the sand, the wind stirred the trees, and the song of a nightingale thrilled through her, giving her a peace and contentment she'd never known.

Zack turned and faced her. "You know, little one, I like the way you wear that Indian headdress. Kind of jaunty." He gave her a mocking half smile. "Just like you!"

She laughed deep in her throat, thinking how different his reaction to her appearance was, compared with Oliver Loomis's. "You approve, then, of my free spirit?"

"Always have and always will," he answered lightly. "Just look what you've accomplished by being your own person." He examined her face, his approving gaze as soft as a caress.

Her heart jolted at how wildly handsome he was. She moved closer, then smiled impishly, thinking that "wildly handsome" was not exactly the right phrase to describe a sober Pilgrim man!

He returned her smile. "It's good to be alone with you, my dearest." He touched her cheek. "What a life we're going to share in this new land!"

Their eyes locked, and in the silver-gray twilight she could see her tiny image reflected in Zack's black eyes. He bent and gently kissed her, and his strong embrace felt natural and right. She wrapped her arms around his neck.

Zack looked into her tawny brown eyes. For a moment all they heard was the sound of the waves rushing to meet the shore. Then Zack kissed away her salty tears, and as his lips touched hers again, Merrie knew, standing on the shore of this fine new land, that the stowaway girl had come home.

Coming next from Sunfire: NORA, who lost everything in the great San Francisco earthquake, except her courage to love.